AMOS AND ANDY:

a White Perspective on Black America

DAN SULLIVAN

Copyright © 2015 Dan Sullivan
All rights reserved
First Edition

PAGE PUBLISHING, INC.
New York, NY

First originally published by Page Publishing, Inc. 2015

ISBN 978-1-68139-528-9 (pbk)
ISBN 978-1-68139-529-6 (digital)

Printed in the United States of America

Dedication

This book was written in the hope that my grandchildren, Jackson and Nicholas, would live in a country that was finally free of the shackles of racial animus and that the dream of Rev. Dr. Martin Luther King that black, white and all children would be treated by the content of their character and not the color of their skin.

In Gratitude

Thanks to Judi Finkle and Phil George for their motivation and continued support for this project.

Contents

Prologue 9
Chapter 1: My Introduction to Race 11
Chapter 2: Growing Up White 15
Chapter 3: Genesis 25
Chapter 4: Happy Days 31
Chapter 5: The Day JFK Died 35
Chapter 6: Thank You, Lyndon 42
Chapter 7: Senator Moynihan and AFDC 54
Chapter 8: Jesse Jackson's Coming-Out Party 60
Chapter 9: The Scourge of Black Hope 64
Chapter 10: Adam Clayton Powell to Charlie Rangel 69
Chapter 11: Who Is My Father? 74
Chapter 12: Jackie and Malcolm 78
Chapter 13: The Oprahfication of America 93

Chapter 14: The Supremes to Gangster Rap 97

Chapter 15: Hollywood 102

Chapter 16: Media Bias 109

Chapter 17: The Great Equalizer 118

Chapter 18: The Power of Faith 141

Chapter 19: Hope and Change 145

Chapter 20: Black Heroes and Villains 152

Chapter 21: White Heroes and Villains 191

Chapter 22: The Specter of Ferguson 212

Chapter 23: Reconciliation 216

Epilogue 221

Prologue

Today, America is more racially divided than at any other point in my sixty-nine years. I would like to present a different approach to the problem of racial harmony. I am neither a PhD nor a talking head from television or talk radio but rather a simple average white person. People have listened to enough opinions from all sides of the debate. I have no agenda but to lay facts before you for your consideration. You then decide whether I am creating a good starting point to engage in meaningful dialogue.

This project has been driven by an abiding belief that this country's treatment of its citizens of color has been both shameful and abhorrent. However, we as a nation should be able to rise above our past sins to get to a better future for all. I have not lived in a cocoon and would not be considered a cockeyed optimist by those who know me best. My life experiences, observations, and recommendations will strike you as quite different from what you hear daily about racism in America.

The title is a throwback to my childhood. *Amos and Andy* was a successful radio show in the 1940s and a very popular television show on CBS from 1951 to 1953. It reflected a time when black people were considered second-class citizens but had a sense of themselves and their community far better than today. Families were strongly bonded through religious beliefs, and they struggled to survive bitter subjugation by a white establishment. Education was stressed and valued by hardworking parents. Children were nurtured by a strong sense of extended family and community.

The cowardice shown by white people to be open and frank in discussing race today is appalling. Many are intimidated by the real threat of being labeled a racist for speaking the truth. No productive dialogue can be achieved when reality is subordinated to hypersensitivity. There are many outspoken black citizens who call for changes in the black culture: illegitimacy, fatherless homes, glorification of sex and violence in gangsta rap music, and rampant crime against black people in the poorer communities. These honorable people are called Uncle Toms by parasites feeding off of racial discord. Therefore, how can a white person hope to be legitimately heard? I have no such fear or concern because of my age, circle of acquaintances, and my family's awareness of the sincerity of my motives.

I hope that you will be entertained and informed.

Chapter 1:

My Introduction to Race

I grew up in a very religious family. We went to church weekly and listened to the same messages from the pulpit about the golden rule of loving thy neighbor as you would yourself, a simple yet very powerful creed. It was also a very strong period of patriotism with the culmination of World War II and the onset of the Korean War. Those two forces dominated my formative years. I had as models a priest and nun on my mother's side of the family, and all of my uncles served in the wars. People of color were nowhere to be found in my hometown of Manchester, New Hampshire, during my early childhood.

My earliest recollection of seeing a black person was on television in a boxing match. There was a weekly ritual of going to my grandfather's home every Friday evening after supper to watch the *Friday Night Fights*. My uncle, Joe, and his family were also regulars. I do not remember the fighters involved, but one was white and the other was black. My mother, aunt, and grandmother remained in the kitchen while the men and young boys gathered around a television with a very small screen. The boxers were introduced by the ring announcer and then it started. All three men (my father, uncle, and grandfather) began referring to "the darkie" in awful terms and rooted that the white guy would beat the hell out of him. As luck would have it, the black fighter knocked the white guy out early in the fight, and they were disgusted with the white fighter's performance. They were all drinking beer before and during the fight, and it seemed to ruin the evening for all. I believe that I was about four years old, and I had never seen my father in this light before. I dared not ask or say anything but simply absorbed it. I understood that when my father drank to excess he took on a different persona, and my mother and I readily knew that it was a time for silence. This particular evening never left my consciousness.

This scene was repeated over and over for years, and as a result I hated going to my grandparents' home. My paternal grandmother was a sweet woman with the proverbial heart of gold, but she was totally subservient to my grandfather. He was never other than kind to me, but I knew him to be a very hard man with his wife and sons. I discovered over time that the views about black people expressed at the *Friday Night Fights* were the norm within my mother's family as well, except for her parents. These were all good people by any reasonable standard and none, to the best of my knowledge, had any personal negative contacts with a person of color upon which to base the hatred and loathing that they expressed.

AMOS AND ANDY: A WHITE PERSPECTIVE ON BLACK AMERICA

In 1951 a new television show appeared on CBS. It had a time slot of 5:00 p.m. (suppertime). The Amos and Andy show become an instant favorite of mine. It was about a group of black people living in Harlem in contemporary times. The lead character was the Kingfish played by Tim Moore, a veteran actor. The Kingfish's goal in life was to constantly separate money from his best friend, Andrew H. "Andy" Brown. Amos was a hardworking cab driver with common sense and a lovely family, and he was a friend to both, but he always tried to keep Andy out of the clutches of the Kingfish's schemes. It was and remains one of the funniest comedy shows of all time. This show portrayed life in the black community of the times. It had black policemen, teachers, nurses, lawyers, businessmen and was almost entirely cast with black actors. I routinely hoped that my father would not come home earlier than five thirty because if he did, he would immediately change the channel and ask what the hell was wrong with me. The show ran for but three years and by all accounts was successful but it suddenly disappeared (more on this in a later chapter). All of the characters presented in this show demonstrated skill, professionalism, and realism. They were the antidote to racist views of the dumb, shiftless (a black custodian nicknamed Lightning was mentally challenged but had a job), and ambitionless black man or woman. They were caring, family oriented, God-fearing people, who were like every other human being trying to get by in the sometimes harsh world. There were no political statements made on the injustices that were out there.

My classmates were all fans of the show and we would replay scenes the next day and laugh our asses off all over again. The Kingfish once sold Andy a trip across the country in a trailer, and they never left Central Park in New

York City. He went so far as to paint the grass outside the trailer blue so that he could convince Andy that they were in Kentucky, the Bluegrass State. The Kingfish's mannerisms and lines were classics. Nobody that I knew saw the show in a negative light. We laughed at the pure humor of the situations and not at the color of the people or the gross stereotypes of Negroes (the euphemism of the era). My mother watched occasionally and had a few laughs. I never heard my mother say a disparaging word about any people of color. I attribute my sense of discomfort about the way people viscerally disliked black people to her attitude that all people were God's children.

I was lucky to have counterbalances to avoid the stereotyping of black people. I understand that those children who have a one-sided presentation of bigotry are predisposed to accept it as valid. The public schools in this country have abdicated responsibility in the area of moral education. A teacher who mentioned the golden rule in a classroom can reasonably fear a complaint from the American Civil Liberties Union. There are also many among us who hear and see overt bigotry and shirk the personal responsibility to confront or at least challenge it.

Chapter 2:

Growing Up White

It is generally accepted as fact that black children are born with a significant disadvantage. It is also assumed today by the vast majority of African Americans that white children are therefore advantaged from birth. I would submit that both are gross generalizations without substantial fact. I was born white to a two-worker family when the norm was the "Leave It to Beaver" type household. Almost all of my friends had stay-at-home moms/homemakers. I was cared for daily by my maternal grandmother in her home from early morning until my mother got home from work in the late afternoon. I had a loving and nurturing home environment during my childhood. When I was five, my hero, my maternal grandfather, a lieutenant on the Manchester Fire Department, died of a heart attack at the age of fifty-three. I had been like an appendage to him, and he treated me like gold. He was bigger than life, and then one morning he was gone. It was one of several exposures to death that I had to deal with in my youth. My grandfather's death prompted my family to move into my grandmother's home after it was split into two separate apartments. On one side were my grandmother, my aunt, and two uncles and the other housed my parents, my newborn brother, and me. We existed as one family of eight in most respects.

I went to school only four blocks away for the next thirteen years. It was a lower middle-class neighborhood with only a few well to do doctors and their families. Their children didn't really associate with my friends and me in our carousing around the streets and playing sports in open fields. We saw them at school but that was it. The only black people that I encountered were a black husband and wife that worked in a dry-cleaning store downtown. They were the Bishops.

My early education was at a private Catholic school that required monthly tuition payments. Nobody was ever given any kind of monetary break, and report cards were never sent home unless tuition payments were current. The nuns had a great system for delinquencies. They called the students that were paid up to receive their cards, and it wasn't hard for children to figure out the status of those who were not called. They were told to see the nun after class. I was in the group to see my teacher after class on more than a few occasions, and I was a consistent A student throughout grammar school. Welcome to Catholic subtlety! The education that was provided was first class but without frills. The nuns were very dedicated teachers, and they always demanded a maximum effort, or hell was the price to be paid. The nuns either made magical strides with the student's improvement, or the student departed for public school. The one caveat was that no student was ever removed if they truly tried to do the work. A part of each school day was dedicated to religion, and this dealt with basics like the meaning of the Ten Commandments, church history, and the types of sin that required acknowledgement and penance. They always combined morality with history lessons, and there was very little ambiguity. The world was black and white with grey totally unacceptable. They would have called moral relativism a sin against logic.

The recess periods for the entire eight grades were at the same time each morning and afternoon. Modern educrats would faint if they witnessed what we found to be joyous combat like "ring a leevo" in the schoolyard. This was a tackling game where people tried to get from one side of the schoolyard to the other without being tackled or knocked to the ground by those in the middle. The villains of the school really looked forward to being in the middle to bang heads. It was a badge of courage to try to cross over, and respect was conferred on those who could take the contact. It was a great way to win friends and influence people. Today there would be arrests for such violent behavior; in fact school administrators are outlawing the game of simple tag. The nuns were like military medics attending to casualties with cuts, scrapes, and bloody noses. It was much more violent than the fighting instruction from Ingrid Bergman, as a nun trying to help a bullied child to fight back in the movie The *Bells of St. Mary's*. Bullying, by the way, was dealt with quite simply in those days. The nuns had CIA knowledge of whatever was going on in and around school. They never shied away from dealing directly with trouble. There were three strikes and you were out.

Strike 1. Confront the offender to secure a sincere apology and impose a form of punishment.
Strike 2. A required visit to the convent with the offender and the parents to include a discussion of the penalties for the transgression.
Strike 3. Good-bye and return your books.

Today people wring their hands and don't want to offend the perpetrator's sensibilities. The victims and their families are given platitudes and excuses.

This code was fairly consistent with most schools of that period. Today, thanks to truly stupid court rulings that children have "rights" in school, all hell breaks loose, and the bullies and obnoxious parents run the schools. Professional educators cower and abdicate their responsibility in promoting moral considerations in their daily teaching schedule. I was fortunate to be taught that teachers were authority figures to be respected at all times at my peril. I was a regular at staying after school and could best be described as a hard case from fifth grade on. The unthinkable today of being made an example of before the entire school became routine for me. Ninety-nine percent of all discipline I received was earned, and the remaining 1 percent didn't seem to matter to my parents.

Grades were easily achieved, but I was often bored to distraction in class. Truancy was not an option because there were truant officers roaming the city streets in unmarked vehicles. Their sole purpose was to round up truant students and bring them to school or sometimes directly to their parents. Had I been caught absent from school, my parents would surely have used the orphanage option threat (not a good option if you had a brain). Attention Deficit Disorder would have been my diagnosis by today's standard for hyperactivity in class. The reality is that kids who are in this state of mind need firm and consistent discipline rather than drugs prescribed by psychological quackery. It is hard to imagine what my life would have been without the kicks in the ass that I received from my parents and teachers.

Athletics played another major role in my life from the age of three when I was brought along by my father to be the batboy for semiprofessional baseball teams that he played for. The camaraderie, humor, and hard work exhibited by competitive adults served as a great example for me. The lessons of baseball fields, hockey rinks, football fields, and gyms stuck with me to this day. Perseverance, a strong work ethic (practice like you want to play), teamwork, and never, ever quitting have been hallmarks for achievement for generations. My father was a very good athlete, but what most stood out about him was his mental and physical toughness. He never backed down or quit trying at whatever he took on.

One evening, as part of a Fourth of July Celebration, a local all star baseball team, including my father, was scheduled to play an exhibition game with a team called the Indianapolis Clowns. I was about eight years old and was the batboy for the Manchester team. When the other team arrived in their dugout, I was stunned. They were all Negroes, and I asked my dad about it, and he told me that they were a barnstorming team that traveled all over the country to play teams like his. You have to go back in time to understand that the Boston Red Sox were an all-white team at that time. The Red Sox were not great, and in fact they were pretty poor in talent. The Clowns took infield and outfield practice before the game, and they did things I had never seen before.

They were flawless in handling ground balls, and their arms were like lasers. The Manchester players were in some awe as well, remarking that if they had a good pitcher the locals would be in real trouble. Nobody wants to be humbled in front of their home fans. The game began, and the pitcher was not going to be the show. His job was to throw strikes but not overpower the locals. The show was going to be about their defense and hitting. There were some derogatory comments by most players in our dugout about the Clowns. There was some false bravado about what they would do to these clowns. It became clear after two innings that these were no clowns and that only the score differential was in doubt. These guys were not only good; they were great at every position. They looked, in every way, like professionals. They hit the hell out of the ball and had several home runs, but they put on a total exhibition of baseball. They bunted for hits, they bunted to sacrifice runners, some ran like the wind, and others had muscles never seen on white players. As superior and dominant as they were, the Clowns did everything with a smile and good humor. They allowed obvious walks to some batters to demonstrate how smoothly they could execute a double play. At one point at the start of an inning a Manchester player hit a ground ball to their third baseman. He stepped on third, threw to second, and the second baseman pivoted for a triple play even though there weren't any runners on base. The crowd roared in amazement. I never recalled the final score, but it was truly no contest as to the quality of the teams.

After the game, all the smiles on the Clowns' faces disappeared. They had acted well, but there were no handshakes, and only their fee needed to be collected. I heard some of our players denigrating their abilities, and even at my young age

I asked myself what game could they have been watching. My father was upset on the way home because he caught six innings and thought that Manchester's pitchers didn't try hard enough, and even worse, he had gone hitless. I was again perplexed because their players could easily have humiliated his team if they chose to. They did not because that would have lessened their chances to play in other communities. I knew nothing about Negro League baseball or the blatant racism that permeated all professional sports, but I did know that night that I had seen players far better than were on the roster of the beloved Boston Red Sox, and I was only a child. It was a quiet ride home because I knew enough to keep my thoughts to myself. The moral of this anecdote is that even at a young age I was able to view people of other colors than my own as having talents well beyond those of my race. How could I know any more without even having spoken to one of them?

The next racial experience I had was when I was twelve. My Uncle Jerry (my mother's twin brother) was living in New Haven, Connecticut, and he worked for H. P. Hood as a residential milk delivery man. He had invited the entire Tellier family to his home for Easter. We all went, and he had a two-bedroom apartment on the second floor of a three-story tenement with eleven guests. To say that it was crowded would be a gross understatement, but it worked. The day after my family got there, my father and I were invited to go see his delivery route in the city on a Saturday morning. He took us to a Negro neighborhood that was in gross disrepair with trash on the sidewalks and in the gutters. The sight was appalling, and my uncle elaborated on the conditions with a steady sprinkling of racial epithets. He informed us that the prime staple for Negro families was bread and milk. Then he noticed a shiny Cadillac in front of a dilapidated tenement, and he used a word I had never heard before. He said that Jigaboos liked to drive nice big cars while their families existed on bread and milk. He was a racist by any standard, and he viewed himself superior even though he was a poorly paid milkman, barely able to provide for his family. He was fortunate to have a loving, tolerant, and selfless wife, my aunt Barbara. Jerry's history had been that of an incorrigible youth. He was sent to boarding school in Canada and got expelled for delinquency. Upon his return home, he was committed by a court to a youth work camp for juvenile delinquents. He joined the US Navy at the outbreak of World War II and served in submarines during the entire war. He was discharged, and like many veterans, he had acquired a serious problem with alcohol abuse. He was clearly the black sheep in the Tellier family. His derision of people of color had nothing to do with his personal encounters but rather a follow-the-leader approach at a relatively young age.

This had been a troubling encounter with the sadness of the situation. I could not forget the sight of young and very young children playing in filthy conditions without supervision or apparent adult concern. It ran counter to my view of Christian charity and fairness. I left New Haven bothered by both the horrific human condition I had seen (I had never even heard of slum conditions like this) and the total disgust that I had for yet another family member with such racial hostility, while my father seemed to have no problem with my uncle's attitude or his show-and-tell demonstration.

My education throughout my younger years always stressed the dignity of all of God's children. Sermon after sermon, priest after priest always promoted Jesus's love for the downtrodden and the sanctity of life. They promoted charitable endeavors and fund-raising in the schools to include African missionary work. We routinely had African priests and nuns visit our diocese in the summer months to help with the plight of African children through separate collections at each mass. I saw it firsthand as an altar boy. The Catholic Bishops' Relief Fund had as its primary mission to help the poor from all races. To the best of my knowledge none of my childhood friends had racist attitudes, and that could not be said of their parents. We enjoyed our lives and were more interested in sports, going to the beach or the lake on weekends, and hoping for the best with our school grades. There was no time for bigotry. In the interest of full disclosure, we all heard and told jokes about ethnic groups and races. In the 1950s this was a genre of comedy that permeated the culture. Some people were offended, but most struck back in an even funnier way. I was a dumb Mick or a dumb Frog when neither applied. Others were Polaks, Guineas, Krauts, or all of the other names now viewed as horrific slurs. The truth is that we all got along much better then. Today's culture of political correctness has bred more tension and less empathy and understanding. I went to the YMCA (Young Men's Christian Association) as a child, and I became friends with kids from every ethnic group in the city of Manchester. Nobody was resented for their faith or ethnic background. It was truly a melting pot for children throughout the city. None of my neighborhood friends ever joined the YMCA or Boys' Club, and they missed out on a tremendous exposure to a whole new set of acquaintances and potential lifelong friendships. I am eternally grateful to my mother for her decision to enroll me in both programs in spite of discouragement by family and our local priest.

The net result of all of this is that anyone can overcome negative exposure to racist attitudes. One need only open their eyes and heart to reality. This applies to all races and not just white people. How can anyone with a sense of decency and fairness deny the tenet stated in the Declaration of Independence that *all* men and women are created equal with the right to life, liberty, and the pursuit of happiness? We long ago dispensed with the notion that people of color were other than human beings.

Chapter 3:

Genesis

Slavery appears to be understood by most to be the immediate cause for black racial animus against white people to this day. There seems to be this great divide between the views of both races on the merit of this argument. Almost 150 years have passed since the Emancipation Proclamation was issued by President Abraham Lincoln, a Republican, and yet black people in some circles insist that they continue to be subjugated by whites. People like me are puzzled by this phenomenon. We look around and see all kinds of signs of black success in business, politics, media, entertainment, sports and world culture. The radical black psychology does not allow for success or stress positive achievement by their black brothers and sisters. To do so would eliminate their own sense of self-importance.

The axiom that those who do not recall history are doomed to repeat its mistakes applies here. The American slave trade was predated by centuries of slavery. The conquerors of the world were notorious for making their vanquished enemies (men, women, and children) into slaves of all varieties. Simply look back to the bondage of the Hebrew nation at the hands of the Egyptians. The Roman Empire enslaved the world as it was known. Over time all of these people became free and did not appear to maintain the shackles of their oppression. They became independent and free to create their own governments, social order, and societies. The notion that black people could not do the same has to be a racial slur in and of itself. This stereotype has been refuted in all the fields of human endeavor. I will try to present a historical perspective to make the case that slaves were capable of overcoming great odds, and many white people throughout history have found slavery and discrimination based on color to be repugnant and evil. There were, however, entire classes of white people wedded to the notion of Negro inferiority.

The first African slaves were brought into colonial Virginia in 1619. Northern congressional leaders in 1787 attempted to ban slavery in new American territories and secured a ban on African slavery that would become law in 1808. Eli Whitney's invention of the cotton gin in 1793 set in motion an increased demand for cheap slave labor for the production of cotton throughout the American South. This produced ongoing disagreement between representatives from slave states and those adamantly opposed to slavery from the North. These tensions continued to be exacerbated until the breakout of the Civil War in 1861. The period from 1793 through 1860 was marked by three separate slave rebellions. The first was led by Gabriel Prosser, an African American blacksmith. The outbreak was soon dispatched, and he was summarily hanged in Virginia in 1800. The second revolt was organized by Denmark Vesey in 1822 in South Carolina. He was an African American carpenter, who had bought his freedom years earlier. This revolt was quickly routed with Denmark, and thirty-four other summarily adjudged conspirators hanged. The last insurrection in 1831 was led by Nat Turner, an enslaved African American preacher, in Virginia. This time the casualties on both sides mounted. Nat Turner and fifty-six of his followers were executed for killing sixty white people, and an additional one hundred more black deaths were attributed to the insurrection. In the aftermath, another two hundred black people were murdered in reprisals by local militias. The net result of these uprisings was the imposition of harsher slave laws by the slave states, but it clearly demonstrated the courage and overwhelming desire of Negroes for freedom against impossible odds. A life in slavery was determined to be more intolerable than death. The deep South today has black congressmen, newly elected senators, and women governors and leaders of academic institutions but little is made of such a significant change in the body politic.

Many Americans in the Northern states found slavery to be an abomination against God. In 1831 their public outrage manifested itself in print. William Lloyd Garrison published "The Liberator", an abolitionist newspaper, whose sole purpose was to attack all elements of slavery in the United States. He was a New Englander and resident of Newburyport, Massachusetts. In 1846, David Wilmot, a congressional Democrat from Pennsylvania, attempted to ban slavery from all territory gained from the Mexican-American War. The vote failed due to the significant majority enjoyed by the slave holding states of the South. In 1852. Harriet Beecher Stowe, a white woman and resident of Brunswick, Maine, wrote and published *Uncle Tom's Cabin*, which was soon read by millions. It was the story of the travails of slaves seen for the first time by all in its starkest reality. She also was a strong member of the abolitionist movement.

The darkest day in United States Supreme Court history came in 1857 with the infamous Dred Scott Decision, which declared that congress could not enact any law to ban slavery in any state, and even worse, it went so far as to declare that slaves were not citizens of this country even when born here. This set in motion even more fervor on the part of Northern abolitionists to destroy slavery and states that supported it. A man from Illinois determined that he should run for the US Senate and that man was Abraham Lincoln. He ran against the incumbent senator, Stephen A. Douglas, a Democrat. They both agreed to debate the issues in the campaign at several predetermined sites. These debates became of significant historical importance. Lincoln, the ardent opponent of all aspects of slavery, and Douglas, the champion of the unthinkable today, with his unequivocal support of the Dred Scott decision. Mr. Lincoln lost the election, but his passion and constant references to the Declaration of Independence in the debates had already fed into a firestorm of righteous indignation in the free (nonslave) states.

A white man named John Brown, viewed by historians as America's first homegrown terrorist, was a deeply dedicated abolitionist. He openly proclaimed that human beings held in slavery would never be freed without force against the slave states. In 1859 he began random attacks against people that he determined were involved in the bondage of slaves. He set forth on a plan to arm black people to form an army of liberation to attack local and even federal forces upholding slave laws. He and his men attacked and seized a federal weapons armory in Harper's Ferry, Virginia, as phase one of his bold plan to inflict chaos and damage in the deep South. The ultimate irony is that federal troops under the command of Colonel Robert E. Lee (yes, the same General Robert E. Lee who surrendered all Confederate forces at Appomattox, Virginia, just six years later) captured John Brown and brought him to justice. The avenging abolitionist was hanged for treason.

Abraham Lincoln may have been a loser in Illinois politics, but in 1860 he was elected President of the United States. This sent a clear message to slave states. Lincoln had become even more strident than his rhetoric in the 1858 debates. The States of the Confederacy was formed in 1861 based on the knowledge that more and more slave states were becoming isolated from real power in economic and political terms. This signaled the oncoming clash that ushered in the Civil War at Fort Sumter, South Carolina, on April 12, 1861. The Army of the Confederacy attacked and laid siege upon this US fort in the Charleston, South Carolina, harbor.

I do not wish to go through the Civil War in detail, but I wish to point out some items of interest:

*It was fought over 150 years ago.
*The Union troops were poorly prepared for the war and were mostly white conscripts, and their leadership was very poor at the outset.
*The sacrifices of both Union and Confederate troops resulted in the bloodiest war in US history in terms of killed and wounded. There was no accounting for collateral damage to civilians in those days.

*The Emancipation Proclamation freeing all slaves was signed by President Lincoln in 1863 during some of the darkest days of the war for the Union side.
*The Confederacy could never sustain itself over a long war with the might of the Union's industrial and manufacturing strengths.
*The end came with destruction throughout the South, while Northern cities remained largely unscathed.

Today, most young adults have no clue of when the Civil War was fought, and I dare say they could care less (this includes both blacks and whites). We can't even imagine what this country would have been like without the courage, tenacity, and religious beliefs of Abraham Lincoln. His reward for this was his assassination by John Wilkes Booth, a Confederate sympathizer, shortly after the war ended in 1865.

On June 19, 1865, the last slaves (250,000) were finally freed in Texas (two weeks after the rest of the country). The thirteenth amendment to the US Constitution abolished slavery forever in these United States in 1865.

My education in grammar school at St. Anthony's was in depth on this issue. The nuns made no bones about their sympathies for all of the oppressed. Negroes had been treated horribly before and well after the war in the period called Reconstruction. The nuns' zeal and commitment to human justice greatly influenced my thoughts on this subject.

Chapter 4:

Happy Days

The television show *Happy Days* was very popular in the mid-1970s because it captured the period of the 1950s and early 1960s as a time of mostly good fun for all. I was a product of that era and still cherish it as perhaps the best time of my life in spite of my father's death in 1961. My high school years had great music, sports, and girlfriends with the related emotional issues. School had little priority when compared to those mentioned even though my mother demanded academic excellence. Baseball was my first love, and that brought my attention to one of the greatest pioneers in bringing about racial respect if not equality, Jackie Robinson. One has to remember that no nationally televised National League baseball games were broadcast in our area of the country. Only the local market team's games were covered (in my case that meant only the Boston Red Sox and their American League foes). The World Series was huge in those days, eclipsing all other sports stories of each year. Then *boom*, Jackie Robinson of the Brooklyn Dodgers flashed onto the small, black and white TV screens across this country. He and his Dodgers team were taking on the greatest franchise in baseball history, the New York Yankees. No Negro player had ever even participated in a professional Major League Baseball game let alone be a starter in a World Series game. He dazzled this vast audience with total skills rarely seen in one player. He hit for average, hit with power, showed great defensive skill, and could run the bases as never seen before by white spectators on such a stage. I was an intense Yankees fan, but I sat there and couldn't help but think back to that Indianapolis Clowns game that I had witnessed years earlier. He stole everything but my beloved Yankees' gloves. This began a personal love affair with Jackie Robinson the player, the man, and the race pioneer. At that time I had no clue about the personal hardships that he and his family had to endure to get to this point in time. I was an avid reader of national baseball magazines, but I never saw any real coverage of this unbelievable story. His achievements could not have happened without the full support of two white men, Walter O'Malley, the team's owner, and Branch Rickey, the general manager. Remember, no other owner or GM in baseball would even entertain such a bold move. In spite of Jackie's obvious successes, the baseball community was very, very slow to embrace integration in either professional league.

My personal experience during high school with black people was very limited. I competed in baseball against Frankie Bishop, a three-sport solid athlete at Manchester West High School. He was the son of the Bishop family that I mentioned earlier that worked at Spotless Cleaners. I knew of no one who didn't like and respect Frankie. He was skilled in all sports and was quiet, humble, and friendly. He was a good student, and upon graduation he moved on to Boston University to get his degree and later became a teacher. There were no racial incidents of any kind in our small town in an almost all-white state. The same could not be said of our neighbor to the South, Massachusetts. Some might say, "What the hell then do you know about black people?" My response is simple. I knew that the one person I was most exposed to was contrary to all of the racial stereotypes of bigots. So why would I believe that other black men, women, and children would be any different?

I'm not naïve enough to think that all of my friends felt exactly as I did, but I will tell you unequivocally that there was no open hostility demonstrated. Yes, there were racial jokes as there were ethnic jokes about any nationality on the planet. Everyone was fair game in those days. The fact that I was Irish and attended a French Catholic high school caused me a lot of grief and the term "frog" was not used as a term of endearment.

There was a wave of black entertainers that took the country by storm during the advent of rock and roll. Ray Charles was a giant, and many of us would gather around a television set just to see his performances on a variety of nationally broadcast television shows. Then Chuck Berry, Diana Ross and the Supremes, and Jackie Wilson came along just to name a few. The Motown sound dominated the early 1960s under the management genius of Berry Gordy Jr. Aretha Franklin was the top female singer in the country, and those golden pipes have been with us for decades since. For pure romance, how could anyone touch Johnny Mathis? No one in my circle of friends uttered a derogatory sound when these people or their other talented peers were mentioned in conversation.

Movies had solid performers like Lena Horne and Sidney Poitier, an Academy Award winner for the 1963 movie *Lilies of the Field*. There were other Poitier films that are viewed as classics today: *The Defiant Ones* with Tony Curtis, *In the Heat of the Night* with Rod Steiger, and *To Sir with Love*. The most influential movie of the period, however, was not a blockbuster nor does it even appear anywhere now. It was *Black like Me* in 1964 that starred James Whitmore as a white reporter who darkened his skin color with medication to look like a black man. He then traveled through America's deep South portraying an unemployed black man. His encounters clearly demonstrated the plight of all black men in America at that time. He was no less educated, no less hardworking, no less qualified, and no less human than he was in his white skin, but he was now scorned, humiliated, threatened, and degraded for one reason only—the color of his skin. The movie is based on the book written by John Howard Griffin, a white reporter for a black magazine. The book was published in 1961, and it is must reading for racial sensitivity in schools, but as I said earlier it is rarely discussed anywhere, probably because the author and actor were white. I could not comprehend how such conditions could exist almost a hundred years after the Civil War. I was still a babe in the woods when it came to the realities of racism not only in the South but in most of America.

Chapter 5:

The Day JFK Died

Upon graduation from little St. Anthony's I moved on to Boston College in Chestnut Hill, Massachusetts. I was now being exposed to a rather large university only a few miles from downtown Boston. My arrival at BC quickly opened my eyes to the haves and have-nots at the school. I was assigned to a so-called dormitory in Brookline, Massachusetts (a barely rehabilitated four-floor tenement two and a half miles from campus without transportation services) that was predominantly populated by students from middle or even lower middle-class households. This surely was not by accident. We were all paying the same room and board rate as those freshmen in the on-campus dormitories. Resident student women were treated no better than we were. The only black students at BC then were a very few scholarship athletes (one in basketball, an All American, John Austin, and three in football). This small number was out of a full slate of intercollegiate athletics totaling several hundred participants. Less than a handful were African exchange students. The numbers would indicate that the supposed enlightened Jesuits were not about piloting affirmative action programs for minorities nor with offering help to disadvantaged African American students. There were no overt racial actions against any of the black students, but many of the white football players disparaged the efforts and the commitment of the black players. One of the African exchange students always kept to himself and was rumored to be an African prince. One of the particularly stupid football players always complained about this prince's attitude. Another football player told him that the prince's roommate was in class with him and confided that the prince had a blowgun and poison darts that he carried for protection. The dumb one was taken aback and said that this should be reported to the Dean of Residents. You almost have to practice to reach this level of stupidity. We all laughed at his expense and continued with the card game that was in progress. I would also add that the staffing for nonacademic jobs on campus was, to the best of my recollection, exclusively white. I do not recall seeing or knowing of any black professors or teaching assistants of color. There you have my introduction to a respected liberal arts university in the fall of 1963.

On November 22, 1963, the world went into slow motion. John F. Kennedy, our president and local hero, was shot and killed in Dallas, Texas. Everyone knows exactly what they were doing and where they were when they heard the news that the president had been shot, and I was no exception. We were in a biology class in Lyons Hall when somebody in the class had a transistor radio on and passed the word that the president had died. We all walked out of Professor Bernasconi's biology class and went to the quadrangle where many radios were now detailing what happened. Ironically, at the same time, a tall black man was handing out newspapers from the Nation of Islam. He was also debating several students about the tenets of the Nation. It caught my attention, and I listened to the dialogue. The representative from the Nation of Islam was no newsboy. He was intelligent, and he articulated his core beliefs with passion but not anger. The BC boys challenging him were smart alecks and downright rude. Suddenly, campus police arrived and told the black man that he had to leave the campus. He left without any conflict and moved to the main entrance to the school on Commonwealth Avenue. Some of us followed and the debate continued. The teachings of the prophet Elijah Muhammad were presented as follows:

> Black people had to become independent from white people and, in fact, be separated.
> Black men had to free themselves from the bondage of alcohol and drugs.
> Black men had to be prepared to resist violence with violence, if necessary, to protect themselves or their families.
> Black men had to care for their wives and children.
> Black men had to support black brother businessmen in their communities.
> Black men needed to read and know the teachings of Allah in the Koran.

He was challenged on many fronts by his questioners, but he responded directly and unequivocally. I was very impressed that he was against the status quo and called on his brothers and sisters to first respect themselves by not seeking handouts from the white government but to work in their black communities to make a difference. He differentiated his views from anarchists like Stokely Carmichael and H. Rap Brown. He defended the use of violence for the protection of self and family and said to do otherwise would make no sense at all. During the debate someone referred to him as a colored man. He was cool and on point with the response that black is the absence of color and, therefore, white people are colored. He added that white people are always trying to tan every summer to look more like black people. It was a remarkable exchange of ideas. I came away thinking that the perception of black Muslims was not reality and that many of their ideas would be helpful to their brothers and sisters who had not yet embraced this theology. A few days after this encounter, Malcolm X, the spokesman for the Nation of Islam, would say publicly that the assassination of JFK was like chickens coming home to roost because of the violence exported throughout the world by the United States (it was Kennedy himself who signed off on the CIA's assassination of the then president of South Vietnam and later escalated the level of US forces in Vietnam). A firestorm of media criticism soon erupted, but it did give me and many other Americans significant pause. Remember, this was 1963, over fifty years ago.

People had told me that college was to be the best four years of my life, and I took them seriously. Once I conquered the habit of going home on weekends, I settled into a life of poor class attendance and poker or kitty whist card games. We routinely went to Celtics games on a walk-in basis because, in spite of their record of championships, they were still a black-dominated team in a white racist city. Bill Russell, one of the greatest NBA players of all time, was very outspoken about how badly he and other black teammates were treated in Boston. He presented a distinction that he loved the Boston Celtics but had no illusions about their fans. We also attended many Red Sox baseball games on the cheap because they were terrible back then. They were still a basically all-white team in spite of the integration of baseball in 1948. The owner, Thomas Yawkey, was a documented racist who had a lot of money and hailed from deeply segregated South Carolina. The Red Sox racial discrimination tactics continued into the 1970s. The rest of my free time was engaged in trying to win at cards. Spending money was being provided by two pigeons that a friend of mine and I clipped on an almost daily basis from kitty bid whist games. The poker games went through evenings into morning when we broke for breakfast. Our biggest fear was getting caught and having the Dean of Residents, Father Hanrahan, grab all of the money in sight. No discipline was ever meted out, but he loved the cash bonuses he was making from these little raids. My fortunes were pretty good, and I won much more than I lost, but my grades were abysmal. I managed to scrape by with late-semester heroics, but for two straight years I had to attend summer school at night to make up required courses. My junior year provided electives and that saved the day. Now success was linked to one thing—camping out overnight to do early sign ups for no show or guaranteed grade courses (this has been brought to an art form in current college academia). These formed the basis for a solid, little work, grade point average. My GPA improved, but it marginally raised my dismal performance in the first two years.

There is a scene in the movie *Animal House* where Dean Wormer has all the miscreants of Delta House in his office to tell them that they are all being expelled and that their draft boards have been duly notified. The looks on their faces said it all. I didn't have that kind of dramatic meeting, but in the second semester of my junior year I did receive a notice from my local draft board ordering me to report for my induction physical because my GPA was below the standard. The draft board advised me that I would not be drafted until I was no longer a full-time student. Many of my card-playing friends received similar notices. I reported for my draft physical and was declared to be 1A (fit for military service). That ruined my whole day. The rest of my college life was carefree and love-free. I was spared the drama that my friends were experiencing: career moves, where to live, when to start a family, and a prospective life with the in-laws. My junior summer I worked as a union ironworker and received full journeyman's pay ($5.07 an hour in 1966), which was quite a lot of money in those days. I helped to support my mother and brother as well as taking care of my senior-year expenses. It was difficult and dangerous work, but I learned firsthand how unions operated. My father had been an ironworker for over twenty years, and the business agent gave me an opportunity that wasn't available to most in my circumstances. Unions at that time were basically closed to blacks and Hispanics. Union member conversations left the clear impression that blacks would not be union members in the construction trades any time soon.

My senior year was relatively uneventful. I did dump my date for my senior reception dinner in favor of another woman that I had met. I didn't go to the reception but rather played miniature golf with my newer friend and had a great time. It was a dog thing to do, but at the time I really didn't care. Exams were completed by the first week of May, and I immediately returned to my ironworker status. Graduation was scheduled for the first week of June. I had actually fulfilled my requirements (even though I made it by the skin of my teeth), and I don't even remember the commencement speaker. I was glad to be done and able to be fat, dumb, and happy for a while. *Wrong.* Two days after graduation, I received greetings from no less than Lyndon B. Johnson telling me to report for induction. I had read up on Vietnam and our mission there. It was 1967, and troop strengths were being increased steadily, and it didn't seem like a rosy place to go. I went to the draft board to inform them that I was working full time as an ironworker to support my mother and brother, but I had no political juice, and they denied my requested exemption. No National Guard or Reserve units had openings (again no political juice), so I waited for a revised induction date and received October 16, 1967.

Chapter 6:

Thank You, Lyndon

I reported to the local Armed Forces Entrance and Examining Station at the appointed hour and date, but I got a reprieve to the next day, same time. Wow, I already received a free day that counts toward my two-year draft requirement. When I got home, my mother thought that I had already gone AWOL (absent without authorized leave). She seemed happy to have me home for one more day. On October 17, 1967, I headed by plane to Fort Benning, Georgia, with six other inductees from New Hampshire to start basic training. Thus began a four-and-a-half year stint starting as a basic trainee (private E-1) and culminating with a writing assignment for the Fort Dix, New Jersey commanding general's staff as a (captain O-3). Sandwiched in between was graduating from infantry officer candidate school, graduating from helicopter training, and a tour in Vietnam as a cobra helicopter gunship pilot. My many assignments exposed me to significant interactions with black people.

My assigned bunkmate in basic training was Melad Smith, a black sharecropper's son from Southern Georgia. He said that he had a ninth-grade education but really had no reading or writing skills. He did have one thing, an abundance of common sense. Our platoon of forty trainees was truly integrated with black soldiers from throughout the deep South (I was in the status of a minority as one of seven Northern Yankees). I never totaled it up, but my guess is that our basic training company of 240 trainees was at least 40 percent black, and most of them were seriously deficient in basic reading, writing, and math skills. Many played blackjack and couldn't count to twenty-one, and many white Southerners were equally deficient (my introduction to the expression "poor white trash"). They were suited to be perfect grunts for LBJ (President Johnson's own designation) in the infantry. Melad and I got along well, and we helped each other throughout the training cycle. We also spent casual time describing what our lives had been like before being drafted. He was as laid back as could be, while I was a typical type-A personality. Melad offered me the best counsel that I ever received when he encouraged me to opt for OCS (officer candidate school). He pointed out that advancing with some control over my destiny had to be better than shipping off to Vietnam, where we were most likely headed as infantry grunts. I had refused that option earlier at the reception station upon my arrival at Fort Benning but agreed ultimately with his rationale.

While in basic during the first four weeks, we were restricted to our company area (the barracks for 240 trainees and the company orderly room for our company commander and his staff) except to go to church on Sundays. It was remarkable how religious everybody became each Sunday. However, this led to my only real distasteful encounter with racism within my own religious community. My first trip to mass after many, many moons of being away was entirely soured. As people advanced to the communion rail in a very small chapel, I became aware that only whites moved forward and only after they had received the host did black people move up to receive communion. I was dumbstruck and became angry. I waited after mass to speak with the Catholic chaplain. He tried to explain that this was only a small accommodation. I responded, "An accommodation to whom?" He explained that we were in the deep South and that the Catholic Church was not strong in this part of the world. I told him that I was offended both as a barely practicing Catholic and as a human being. I admit that I returned the next three weeks and showed no protest or solidarity with the black folks who were being discriminated against. It was cowardly on my part, but when you're a private E-1, you learn quickly not to rock the army's boat. There was not a hint of discrimination by our superior noncommissioned officers or our commanding officer, a Filipino captain, during our nine weeks of basic training.

Upon completion of basic, I moved on to advanced infantry training (AIT) at Fort Dix, New Jersey, where a whole new experience awaited me. Our new training company had the dregs of the inner cities of the area (both white and black). These were not patriotic individuals but in fact miscreants of the worst kind who got to choose the army over jail time. There were constant fights, threats, and uneasiness in the barracks. Add to this a drill sergeant, Sergeant Hufnagel, who might have been the worst human being that I encountered in my entire military experience, and you have eight weeks of purgatory above and beyond the training demands. I made it through by sheer avoidance and guile. Another new element for me here was my first encounter with Hispanics who were from Puerto Rico. They had little or no English skills and kept entirely to themselves. It was clear that the troublesome blacks and the white trash did not like them one bit. They were simply more cannon fodder for the war machine, and I had no relationship with them because of the language barrier. I was actually thrilled to be heading back to infantry officer candidate School (OCS) at Fort Benning, Georgia. I was relieved and somewhat happy that I would be returning to a post that I was at least familiar with.

My six months at Infantry OCS had but one significant racial component. Shortly after our arrival, a cataclysmic event took place on April 4, 1968, in Memphis, Tennessee. Martin Luther King Jr. was assassinated, and all of Fort Benning was put on full alert.

I knew of Doctor King's work in civil rights because he studied at Boston University, and he had been active in the civil rights struggle in the Boston area. He had received his doctoral degree from Boston University. This event came as a shock to everyone, but since Doctor King and his family lived in Atlanta, the military thought that all hell would break loose not far from us. We talked among ourselves, and nobody was itching to get on a truck to patrol the streets of Atlanta. Riots began breaking out in major cities all over the country when the news spread. For better or worse, the governor of Georgia at the time was Lester Maddox, an avowed racist and former Ku Klux Klansman. Lester immediately went on television and proclaimed martial law, bringing in the Georgia National Guard and Georgia State Police. He even went further and stated unequivocally that he had ordered that looters be shot on sight. I was frankly dumbfounded by this statement, but it worked; there was no violence of any significance. Atlanta survived as few cities with predominantly black populations had. I had escaped another potential nightmare. My feelings were similar to those at the time of JFK's death. Why would this man espousing peaceful protests against the unbearable conditions of his race be struck down by an assassin's bullet? The aftermath unfortunately resulted in more hardship in the communities that were burned down over the black inhabitants' frustrations.

In August of 1968, I became a commissioned second lieutenant, and this supposedly conferred upon me the status of gentleman. The reality was that I could now expect to be treated like Rodney Dangerfield until I became a worthy first lieutenant. My new assignment would be at Fort Riley, Kansas, as a mechanized infantry platoon leader. Fort Riley wasn't even known to me or my fellow OCS graduates. Kansas's auto plates had a little saying on them, "Midway USA," and the joke was that it was to the point because we were now a thousand miles from anywhere.

I reported in at my unit and met my soon to be roommate, First Lt. William "Bolo" Campbell. I was now a part of the Rocks of Chicamagua Battalion, and I was in charge of four armored personnel carriers and forty-four soldiers and noncommissioned officers. Bolo Campbell, shortly after my arrival, invited me to fill an open roommate spot at his apartment in Manhattan, Kansas (home of Kansas State University). There were two other roommates: Major Peter Jengo, a dentist, and First Lt. James Mitchell, who happened to be black. This was a pretty good foursome. We played cards, went out to dinner, and generally hung out together. All was good until Oct. 16, 1968, when while watching the summer Olympic Games from Mexico City, Tommie Smith, an American black track star, had set a record for the 200-meter dash, winning the gold medal; and John Carlos, another black teammate, had won the bronze medal. Then the world went upside down. The two American athletes were on the awards stand, and as the American national anthem began, both black Americans bowed their heads and raised black gloved fists in the air to symbolize black power. Jengo was the first to go off into a tirade, while James just sat there quietly. I chimed in and asked James what he thought of the scene and he replied that "It was about time that someone stood up for black people in America." All civility went out the window; three white guys were attacking Mitchell for what we felt was an affront to our nation. It got very ugly, and we each departed the room. James was a graduate of Western Kentucky and was very well read with a degree in US History. He was easy going, but this had struck a nerve, and we had exacerbated it by our lack of knowledge of what it felt like to be black in America. We were all from New England, and he grew up in the South, so what the hell did we really know? The cold war lasted about a week, and Mitchell was planning to find other living arrangements. Then the firebrand of the three antagonists (a self-proclaimed liberal) Jengo, offered a sincere and emotional apology to James with Bolo and me following suit. There was no immediate love fest, and tensions remained for several weeks. All of us had learned a lesson about sensitivity and friendship. James and I left for other assignments in the next eight months with Mitchell being the only one to immediately head to Vietnam. This experience was the only thing of value that I got from being stationed at this godforsaken area of the country. I was then off to helicopter flight school and later Vietnam.

My flight-school experience was devoid of any real racial exposure until I got to the second phase in Savannah, Georgia, at Hunter Army Airfield. There were no black aviators in my flight-school class, and to be perfectly honest, I do not remember seeing any throughout my training or in Vietnam. Maybe it was a closed shop because of education or a lack of prior flight experience. I honestly don't know.

I did have firsthand knowledge that Savannah was tough on black people. There was subtle segregation with private-card (the club issued membership cards to whites on the way in), white-only night clubs, and I do not remember seeing any black police of any kind off post. There were even well-known small white-only communities around Savannah where blacks were not welcome and even threatened openly by billboards. Inner black Savannah was reminiscent of what I had seen in my childhood experience in New Haven, Connecticut. My encounters in neighboring South Carolina were even worse. Black people there lived in shanties on cement or stone blocks, and as employees they were openly mistreated and demeaned. I stopped for gas once while returning to Savannah from my home up North on the main highway (Route 17) in South Carolina, and a young black man came to fill me up. He did so and I gave him a twenty-dollar bill (gas was very cheap then). Suddenly this fat old redneck came out and began yelling at me for giving the black man my payment. I couldn't believe it, and I shouted back at him not to dare yell at me and that maybe he should have gotten off his fat ass to come out and serve me himself. The black man was visibly scared of this guy, so I let it go. The clown then took the money and later sent a white guy out with my change. Incidents like this were why I carried a gun under my seat throughout my assignments in the deep South. I had army tags on my bumper, and the car had Georgia plates at the time.

I had a serious arthritic episode that landed me in and out of the hospital for a little over six months, and in my year assigned there it never really got any better.

It is with this understanding that I cannot believe the treatment that Clarence Thomas, a native of Savannah, and the only black sitting judge on the US Supreme Court, took from his own race during his confirmation hearing. By the way, can anyone name a Democratic president that even nominated a black man or woman for the Supreme Court other than Thurgood Marshall in 1967? He is the only other black Supreme Court justice in history. The Clarence Thomas story has never been told in full in our public schools, and that is shameful. Compare his daunting travels to the Supreme Court with those of our current president and tell me who had the rougher road.

I finally completed cobra helicopter gunship school in August of 1970, and it was now off to the Republic of South Vietnam. I can remember thinking while on the last leg of the trip from Yokota, Japan, to Saigon that I might just be the dumbest bastard on the planet. I had declined a disability discharge because of my arthritis. The press then was routinely decrying the morale of the troops and particularly the racial strife. I witnessed some of this firsthand, and although it certainly existed, it was nowhere near the level stated in media coverage. It wasn't near as much about black versus white as it was everyone versus the US Army. Everyone in the country by 1970 knew that the war was a very sick joke, and troops were dying and being maimed for life for absolutely nothing. The common enemies for whites and blacks alike were boredom, drugs, dealing with the heat, the monsoon rain and the clear fact that the South Vietnamese could have cared less about who ruled them.

My unit was relatively busy trying to support Republic of Vietnam ground troops on a daily basis. We had internal problems with a relatively few malcontents, some of whom were black. Our pilots were generally on twenty-four-hour-a-day call for emergencies in the Mekong Delta region, and that often included Medevac protection. A few black guys seemed to enjoy yelling obscenities and terms of endearment like "go out and die, pigs" while we ran to our aircraft, and this got our attention.

Our commanding officer, Major Jeremiah Daley, was the best person I ever knew in the army. He developed a process for dealing with nonperforming soldiers (black and white). He had a connection with somebody in personnel assignments, and if someone really crossed the line, they could expect to spend the remainder of their tour atop a listening post. This meant that they were helicoptered in with bad guys expected to be at the base of the mountain they were on top of. Not a good position to be in.

Recreational drugs could be bought within our airfield perimeter, and literally anything could be purchased in downtown Can Tho City. The drug dealers kept their equal-opportunity sales goals in mind for there were no barriers of race, color, creed, or rank. It was appalling how easy it was for enlisted people to get wasted. There were more drug deaths in Can Tho than war casualties. What a waste of lives for *nothing*!

I returned to the United States and was posted at Fort Dix again, but now I was a basic training company commander. I had now come full circle (trainee to commander). The war was winding down thanks to Nixon's secret plan to end the war. He and his sidekick, Henry Kissinger, cleverly negotiated with the North Vietnamese (how did that all work out for those South Vietnamese that actually trusted those two). A beautiful and peaceful nation, Cambodia, was totally destroyed by our incursion there and brought about the disastrous regime of Pol Pot and the Khmer Rouge. Kissinger (still revered as a genius) and Robert McNamara were truly American war criminals by any fair standard. The blood on their hands stained this country's foreign policy forever, and it's worse today.

The quality of my trainees had not improved much from my last tour there, and the mix seemed to have become even more populated by inner-city African Americans. Overall the vast majority were hardworking and patriotic people. My drill sergeant cadre was led by Sergeant First Class Jorge Rodriguez, with a 50/50 cadre of white and black noncommissioned officer drill sergeants. The one thing we had in common was to provide the best training possible without any prejudice whatsoever. We also shared a view that we would cull out the misfits that could ultimately get people hurt or killed overseas. My problem was that this attitude conflicted with my commanding officer's stated objective to move any and every warm body to graduation. I held to my standard, and in the US Army this was not acceptable, so after one complete training cycle I wound up moving to the commanding general's staff to be one of his writers until I left the service.

Two of us held these jobs. In the ultimate of ironies, my counterpart was Francis Xavier Hiney, a Holy Cross grad and our boss was a black man, Major Frank Myers. Major Myers was very good to both of us, and I managed to stay out of further trouble until I left the army on April 20, 1972.

I learned a lot in the army about myself and about race. It was one of the few bastions of equality in America at the time. Some without knowledge might scoff and complain that black participation in Vietnam was unreasonably skewed. The reality is that statistically 12.5 percent of African Americans fought and died in that war, while 86 percent of their white counterparts died as well (per History.com). That does not square with the complaints of the liberal elite about racial genocide toward black people. As of November 23, 2013, the demographics of all armed services were as follows: 74.6 percent white, 17.8 percent black, and 7.6 percent other in an all-volunteer setting. I still resent the well-to-do that managed to escape their fair share of the Vietnam load. Some of these people who were taken care of politically to avoid service later became "chicken hawks" in the Bush administration that helped get us into wars in Iraq and Afghanistan.

The reality, though, was that blacks were fairly promoted on merit and were true equals of all races in the war. I sat on promotion boards my last year in the army, and the best-qualified list assessments had no pictures or other identifying info available to the panel. Black noncommissioned officers were the backbone of the wartime army, and they still are today. Education was made available to anyone interested in bettering himself. The first black cabinet officer in history and a person of tremendous influence was a product of this culture. He is Colin Powell, a true American hero, and his rise came under Ronald Reagan and George H. W. Bush (both Republicans).

I respected and received respect from people of color who were facing the same trials and tribulations that came with being in the military.

Chapter 7:

Senator Moynihan and AFDC

My first real full-time position after leaving the army was as a claims representative with the Social Security Administration. On a curious note, when I interviewed for the job, one of the three panelists, a middle-aged black man, asked me, "Did you like killing gooks"? This appeared to shock the other two panelists, one of whom was a white woman, but I responded that "I did my job to the best of my abilities as did all of the people I served with." Can you for a moment imagine a white man on this type of panel asking such a racially charged and inappropriate question during a job interview for taking and processing claims from people? I was very offended, but out of character I kept my cool and got the job. I got to know more about this guy in my years with Social Security, and he was not very good at anything. Truth be told, he was viewed as pure tokenism within the Social Security Administration, and in my experience he was not alone.

I was first assigned to a small office in Nashua, New Hampshire. There were but twelve employees, and one was a black woman who became my clerical assistant for the next four and a half years. Eileen Burton was bright, cooperative, helpful, and empathetic with claimants. She worked hard and was always swimming against the tide with our manager, Anthony Longobardi. She was very sensitive and was often in conflict with some of the other ladies in the office over their attitudes and work ethics. She was unable to advance primarily because she was viewed by the manager as a troublemaker! I had several discussions with him about this to no avail. It was abundantly clear that he was prepared to accept her to avoid personnel problems, but she would get nowhere promotion-wise. I was already viewed by many in our office as difficult and demanding, but I should have done more. I could have fought with my manager or tried to convince our assistant manager to act on her behalf. I did nothing, and for that I carry shame to this day.

A claims representative's day called for dealing with people about to retire without being prepared for it financially or emotionally, widows and widowers face a future without their life partners often with minor children and the disabled with all of the issues that one can only imagine. I also came in contact with welfare clients on a regular basis because of their need for social security numbers for themselves or their children. This more than anything else caused me pangs of sorrow but also anger that most of the children that I saw were being condemned to a future of poverty, neglect, and abuse. The Aid to Families with Dependent Children (AFDC) law was seriously flawed legislation, and I was a helpless witness to this ongoing human disaster. The vast majority of AFDC mothers that I encountered were uneducated with little or no child skills. They weren't people who had fallen on tough times but rather people without any ambition or motivation. It sticks with me today how badly I felt for those kids.

The 1935 Social Security Act enacted during the administration of President Franklin D. Roosevelt included Title VI, Aid to Dependent Children. It called for a partnership between the federal and state governments to provide cash assistance to children of parents with little or no income during the great depression. It was a voluntary program for the states with eight of the states opting to decline. The original appropriation by the US Congress was $25 million. This was a part of Roosevelt's New Deal reforms and legislation.

This effort had serious growing pains because the money sent to the states was relatively unconditional, and the states were allowed to rule on eligibility decisions. It became clear over time that Southern states with animus to black people were not applying equitable standards for all eligible people. There were no national standards for eligibility or payments, so much of this welfare assistance was arbitrary. In 1962 the name was changed to Aid to Families with Dependent Children, and it now included grant money for the parent(s) of the children in the same household. An ongoing flaw became the more lenient treatment of the income of a cohabitating person in the household versus a married spouse. The message became clear: don't marry, and the grant amount would be higher; and have more children, and the grant will be larger. Another problem arose from judicial rulings from 1968 through 1970. These eliminated cohabitation as a terminating event, they struck down state residency waiting-period requirements, and they determined that AFDC was a property right that required a due process hearing for reduction or termination (prior to this it was strictly welfare and states could make such determinations based only upon their own eligibility rules).

By the time I came onto the scene, the program was clearly in disarray. We were routinely contacted by state welfare agency fraud units to verify the accuracy of social security numbers, and most did not belong to the AFDC clients. This preceded the computer age, and it was the easiest thing in the world to get a phony social security number. 1976 became the high water mark in dollars spent on AFDC adjusted for inflation at $24 billion. Believe it or not, that was a lot of money back then.

Not only were budgets rising at an alarming rate, but the destruction of the fabric of inner city black communities was clear collateral damage. Out-of-wedlock births were going off the charts for black women. They were grossly disproportionate with the rise of white women out of wedlock births. Everything humanly possible was being done by government to eliminate any stigma of welfare assistance. States were mandated to offer one location for filing welfare-related applications. AFDC-eligible women were given Medicaid for themselves and their children, but this was supplemented further with food stamps. You and I might not want to live like this, but in low-income areas and particularly in inner cities, this appeared to be a ticket to project independence. Add to the mix a boyfriend not reported to authorities, and you've got a clear incentive to get pregnant and continue to get pregnant. Those that argue that this is a minority of the AFDC households simply ignore the data that is overwhelming on this point. Why else would you have generational AFDC clients with so many children? I argue instead that we should create incentives through mandatory work, vocational training, and education requirements (with a general equivalency degree as a minimum).

Senator Daniel P. Moynihan (Democrat-NY) a strong proponent of AFDC, lamented publicly before he died in 2001 that AFDC as it had been created had unforeseen human costs and wasted financial outcomes. President Bill Clinton supported, and with a push from a Republican-controlled US Congress, enacted the Personal Responsibility and Work Opportunity Act of 1996 (one of his major achievements). It called for sweeping welfare reform with bipartisan support. The previous AFDC provisions of the Social Security Act were reformed, and the AFDC provisions were renamed as Temporary Assistance to Needy Families. It placed into federal law the following features:

*Pregnant women within 120 days of pregnancy were eligible for grant money, prenatal care, Medicaid, and food stamp eligibility.
*Maximum lifetime benefits were limited to sixty months with very limited exceptions.
*Recipients must be working or in a job-training program within twenty-four months of eligibility.
*Single parents must participate in work activities at least thirty hours/week
*Two-parent households must participate in work activities between thirty-five and fifty-five hours/week.
*Failure to comply can result in reduction or termination of eligibility.
*Recipients can be called upon to care for children of other families receiving assistance who are working.

The clear goal was to move single-parent households to two-parent households by providing incentives to that end.

It is incredible that it took sixty-one years to require a work component to welfare payments but credit Bill Clinton, one of the greatest politicians ever, for getting it done.

One of the most distasteful elements of welfare is the notion that people who are able to work do not because it is in the recipient's best interest to stay on the dole. This is a gross overgeneralization to black and white mothers alike. However, the argument that more white people receive welfare than people of color begs the question, why aren't the percentages the same? Not only are they not even close, it is a feeble defense that color issues in this area do not exist and that black folks are scapegoated when it comes to federal aid. When one looks at the black culture over the past forty years or more, it is an inescapable conclusion that black young men and women exercise little or no responsibility in sexual matters. The panacea from liberal thinkers was to promote birth control and abortion on demand. Just imagine for a moment what the numbers would be if the numbers of aborted black fetuses were included! Let's look at the infamous octomom who already had six children and then tried for multiple births and succeeded with eight more. She can't support any of them properly, and she has celebrity status. This country isn't going nuts, it is nuts. We have spectacularly paid black athletes who have to be dragged into court to pay overdue child support to not just one woman but several. When events such as these occur, they should be teaching moments for black youth, but when credible black people speak out on the worst of today's black culture, they are dismissed as Uncle Toms.

Chapter 8:

Jesse Jackson's Coming-Out Party

Rev. Jesse Jackson is one of the most polarizing figures in black or white politics. Black people would vote for him for anything, and most white people want him to just go away. His political roots came at the feet of Rev. Dr. Martin Luther King Jr., and he was in Doctor King's presence at the time of his assassination in Memphis in 1968.

Jesse was born out of wedlock on October 8, 1941. He has proven over his lifetime that through education and hard work a black child could achieve his or her dreams. He is truly an enigma to me. He has done heroic things: marching and working for racial equality at the shoulder of Doctor King in the hostile deep South in the turbulent sixties and running for President of the United States in 1983 and again in 1987. He gave the most electrifying speech I have ever heard at the

Democratic National Convention in 1984. The irony is that few people actually listened to the speech because he didn't make his appearance until after 11:00 p.m. The bosses of the Democratic Party that were favored by more than 90 percent of all African Americans decided to put the Rev. Jackson on at the back of the bus. He spoke eloquently and on point to *all* Americans, and I heard his message loud and clear. It was inspiring, conciliatory, hopeful, and passionate. It should be mandatory reading for all students in our schools today. He came across as a man of God with clay feet, and he defined what America should be in the future, and his words still apply today. I have yet to hear a political speaker since with the clarity and humanity shown that late evening. His candidacy was dismissed by pundits and Democrats alike, but he came in third to a very dull Walter Mondale and a seriously flawed Gary Hart.

Reverend Jackson ran again in 1987, but he lost to "the man in the tank," Gov. Michael Dukakis. Jesse became a serious candidate but still waged an uphill battle. He garnered 29 percent of the votes cast in all of the primaries in 1988, while Dukakis received but 43 percent and a distant third came the dynamic (just kidding) Al Gore at 14 percent. So in 1988, twenty years before President Barack Obama's run for the presidency, the Reverend Jackson set in motion the possibility that a black man could be a viable national candidate.

Then there is the not-so-Reverend Jackson. He that embraces the Nation of Islam purely for political purposes well after the Malcolm X assassination at their hands in 1965. The Nation of Islam has clearly been a Jew-hating organization under Elijah Muhammad and the current stewardship of Louis Farrakhan. The common bond that had existed for decades between Jewish and black people was being shredded.

Jesse Jackson only threw fuel on the fire with comments like New York is "Hymietown," a derogatory slur against Jews. Further, he routinely embraced and defended Farrakhan (in Chicago politics that seems to be a litmus test) and has spoken out strongly against the State of Israel. His sense of history was a little deficient because it is the Arab states in the region that made the Palestinians homeless, and it is these same Arab states that have put Israel under siege since it was created by Jesse's favorite organization, the United Nations, in 1948.

To my knowledge he has failed to show the same zeal for the more intense issues that are destroying black people in America: drugs, public elementary and high school educations (or the lack thereof), and black-on-black violent crime in every inner city in this country (particularly in his own hometown of Chicago). Has anyone seen him leading a Selma-type march in Chicago where young black children and adults are being slaughtered daily? There's no money in that for him. Does he attack public education union leadership for the corrupt and decaying educational opportunities available to black children? Does he call out the totally black administered Washington, D.C., school district for being the worst in the United States? When a black person is killed by a white person (regardless of the facts in the case), Jesse is at the forefront. The fact that more black citizens die or are injured at the hands of their own does not get Jesse equally indignant. The issue of drugs is left to people like Jim Brown, the former football great and tireless worker in the area of black economic independence.

Jesse, it would seem, has evolved more into a race hustler and politician (with all the negatives that evokes) than he is a man of the cloth. He has never spoken out on the sanctity of human life unless it pertained to thwarting an execution. He remains mute on the chilling matter of the genocide of black children through horrific African American annual abortion numbers. When has he ever taken on the Democratic Party directly on any issue? When has he ever called for the removal of a black politician who has betrayed his or her constituency including his own son? Do black people feel good about his role in the "lynching" of the innocent white Duke lacrosse players? These questions are on the lips of most white people and rightfully so. He has also betrayed his own wife when he had many sexual affairs with one resulting in his last child being born out of wedlock. As I said earlier, he has demonstrated that he has feet of clay, but he continues to tell others how they should act and live their lives on the white side of the fence. He has lost his credibility with most white people like me. It is a wonder to most that African Americans continue to be of the belief that he is a positive influence for racial harmony. He is a charlatan, a self-promoter, and lines his pockets by maintaining victimization ideology.

Chapter 9:

The Scourge of Black Hope

There is a scene in the classic movie The *Godfather* that describes a meeting of Italian Mafia mob bosses discussing control of the trafficking of narcotics in America. One of the bosses of bosses states that the sale of drugs should be kept in black areas of cities, and he receives quick concurrence from the others in attendance. The timeline for the scene is in the late 1940s.

We move ahead to 2015, more than seventy years later, and find that the single greatest threat to black America is drug trafficking in their communities, their neighborhoods, and their schools. The spiral downward has been carried out not by the white villains that precipitated it but rather by black drug entrepreneurs that took over urban turf and used every means available to solidify their control. What would be the single highest concern of black families today with very young children in their homes? Drug exposure and addiction is surely either number 1 or 1a. Areas of New York City in the early 1970s had the look of bombed-out European cities from World War II. Is it better today? Housing projects intended to give inhabitants a decent place to live with security have become disaster areas for everyone due to drug infestation. Black leaders and politicians on every level wring their hands and come up with zero practical solutions. The rampant corruption of law enforcement at every level is disheartening at the least. The judicial system has equally been compromised and corrupted. Do the names Nicky Barnes and Frank Lucas of New York City, to name a few, ring a bell (the movies *New Jack City* and *American Gangster*, respectively, were biographies of them)? It takes years to put these people away, while horrific damage takes place daily in every city in this country. Drug money affects every element of our society with no end in sight.

It is odd to me that our government could wage a war on Pablo Escobar, the Colombian cartel drug lord, and basically support his execution by Colombian authorities, but we cannot even interdict drugs crossing our borders! The so-called War on Drugs has resulted in more casualties than any of our real wars and to what end? Is there an end in sight? Are the casualties diminishing? Are we safer today? The answer, unfortunately, is *no* to all of the above. So why do we continue this folly ad infinitum? The simple answer is that the money that is going to the various agencies of government is a boondoggle and windfall for all who receive it. You might ask, who are the recipients from this unbelievable cash cow? Here are some examples: FBI, DEA, ATF, Homeland Security, the Department of Education, every state government, every state and local prison official, Border Patrol, politicians who get illicit campaign money, the entire court system, school districts, and on and on.

One of the greatest conservative voices in the last century, William F. Buckley Jr., in the 1970s, called for an end to the War on Drugs because it was a repeat of the failed policies of the prohibition of alcohol from 1919 to 1933. The parallels are striking, but the politicians of the time in 1933 had more common sense. The constituencies were far fewer, and most Americans frankly ignored the law when it came to their personal consumption habits as do most marijuana users today. The point is that the legalization of drugs could eliminate the day-to-day fear that exists for black people of being assaulted or even killed over money to buy the desired product. Drug gang lords would be out of business overnight much as the Al Capone types were in the 1930s. A problem of this magnitude needs plus and minus thought. We have tried the status quo for the past fifty years with disastrous results. The definition of insanity is attempting the same failed solutions over and over while expecting a different outcome! What real impact would such a bold move have within the black communities? How about emptying jails of black men and women serving time for drug-related crimes other than armed assault or murder! Next, schools could be devoid of drug trafficking by students. Lives in the black communities could return to a sense of normalcy with an absence of daily fear of neighbors and drug gangs. The criminal justice system would free up for the relevant application of justice. The wealth and toys amassed by drug dealers would disappear, giving them less of their current appeal. The drug-enforcement lobby would be left with only a tin cup.

Again, some might say you think you're so smart, but law enforcement should know more than you do. Is this the same law enforcement that suffers from rogue cops in every major city because the pool of officers has expanded to include unqualified and, yes, dangerous people? Are these the same people who terrorize innocent people with no-knock assaults by SWAT teams in the middle of the night? Are these the same people who know the untouchable kingpins and can't bring them to justice? Are these the same people who are detested in the black communities for their uneven treatment of people of color? Is this the US Justice Department that allowed hundreds of assault type weapons to be delivered to the Mexican drug cartels under the botched program with the code name Fast and Furious? It truly defies common sense, and yet nobody is willing to admit the obvious from the cartoon sage Pogo: "We have met the enemy and he is us."

Cries of victimization and blatant racism fall on deaf ears of the white majority because they have been desensitized by daily reports of crime and violence in black, low-income areas. They routinely read the names of Hispanics and blacks accused or convicted of drugs and violence. Isn't it odd that you rarely see names like Roy Winston III for drug offenses in the media? Simply put, that is a fact of life in our society. The well-to-do rarely go to jail for drug use or even trafficking! They lawyer up, pull political favors in, or plead out. Does anyone not know of examples of such swells in their personal experience? Maybe I'm too cynical, but I've personally seen it over and over again.

Black people must be accountable as any other segment of the population. The reality is that the deck is stacked against them by a lack of a quality education and economic opportunity. What do you do if you are the sixth child in a welfare mother's family living in public housing and each of your siblings has a different absentee father, and the brass ring is a life of drug crime? The odds are that you do what you think you have to do to survive and escape the life you've been born into. This will never change without the eradication of the economic incentives of a life in the drug trade.

For all the liberals out there who are offended by this, both you and your conservative brethren have produced this mess. It has never been a one-party blueprint to hell. Conservatives are primarily concerned with dollars, while liberals fight every effort to promote individual accountability. Those without political agendas can clearly see roots of problems and possible solutions, but to cobble together meaningful proposals, there has to be a legitimate concern for the people most affected; and that spirit does not exist. You may find this a depressing conclusion, but I would gladly entertain optimism if it was meshed with reality. It is a dire situation, and wishing that it was not so will not help those families that are in desperation over their children's futures. Over a hundred and fifty years ago, very few Negroes escaped from slavery on Southern plantations, yet today millions of black people are enslaved in the inner cities without hope. Education in urban areas of this country is a disaster for nonwhite children. The drug trade and the daily exposure of youngsters to daily crime and violence will not subside without radical intervention. It was not always so. The safety for black citizens in ghetto-like atmospheres has been an ongoing problem for decades. Why can't police forces be bolstered with walking patrols to protect these folks? A stronger police presence and dedication to ensure the protection of all people of color should be paramount in every major city in America to eradicate this scourge of drugs and violence.

Chapter 10:

Adam Clayton Powell to Charlie Rangel

Adam Clayton Powell Jr. was elected to congress in 1945 from the Harlem district of New York City as a Democrat. From 1945 to present, that seat has been occupied by only two people. The second and current congressman is none other than Congressman Charles Rangel, Democrat. These two powerhouses of the US Congress had much in common. They were bright, articulate, good-looking, tenacious about their beliefs, and independent in their white surroundings. The other unfortunate parallel was that their financial greed ultimately resulted in their being censured by their peers. Powell, in fact, was removed by the congress for his financial misdeeds (he later won his suit against the congress for this action in the US Supreme Court but never regained his seat in the House of Representatives). I bring these two forward for examination because it is a mystery to me and most white people that black people continue to support such politicians in spite of clear evidence of their abuses of office. There are countless black and white politicians who have been found to be corrupt. The oddity is that when white politicians are discovered, they are routinely removed by their constituents, but black miscreants are returned to office often by an overwhelming plurality.

Case in point is Washington, D.C., our nation's capital. Its poor black residents live in a hellhole of drug infestation, rampant political corruption, crime, and grossly inferior public education. A former mayor, Marion Barry Jr., was caught on videotape doing drugs and convicted of possession of drugs in a national scandal. He continued to serve as mayor while awaiting trial, and he was ultimately found guilty. Barry served his federal sentence and later was elected to the D.C. City Council and then elected again as mayor. This guy was the bum of bums, and he continued to game the system by conning the electorate over and over. His city is completely governed by a black administration with black municipal officials and a black nonvoting representative in the US House of Representatives. Washington, D.C., is fully funded by the US Congress (the US taxpayers) and what are the results? I would submit that it is anarchy and abject failure.

The latest debacle occurred in 2007 when a new D.C. mayor was elected on a platform of education reform. Mayor Adrian Fenty hired an education reformer, Michelle Rhee, to be the new chancellor of the district's public schools (DCPS). She was a thirty-seven-year-old Korean American and former elementary school teacher with no school management experience. Ms. Rhee put everyone on notice that school performance improvement was to be job number 1. The 50,000 students and 4,300 teachers in the system were going to be held accountable. This was unacceptable at the outset to the teachers union and any nonperforming teachers who stood to get pink slipped. Chancellor Rhee had been given sweeping powers to reorganize schools and dismiss administrators and staff that were not pulling their own weight, and she was comfortable using those powers. In the three years that followed, she was assailed in many quarters, and even though the district had made significant strides toward improvement in testing scores for the first time (a subject of disagreement by the unions and their liberal supporters), she was the lightning rod for demagoguing politicians and school bloodsuckers who attacked anything and everything about her.

Mayor Fenty, to his credit, had staked all of his political capital on her success. He was ousted after one term, and one of the newly elected mayor's first official acts was to fire Chancellor Rhee. There had been a cry of racial insensitivity when this Korean lady had been appointed over another African American candidate. That error has now been corrected with the appointment of another black school superintendent (here we go again)! So now Washington should be able to return to the glory days preceding Ms. Rhee. What a cruel joke on the poor families that turned out to oust a courageous Mayor Fenty and his bold attempt at helping their black children to get a decent education. This was a disgusting blow to a woman whose prime interest was the education of black children and to the entire black community.

For more insight into black voting patterns, we must also examine the recent election of Jesse Jackson Jr. in Illinois. Here we had the son of the Rev. Jesse Jackson serving as a congressman from Chicago who was under federal indictment for misuse of campaign funds for his and his wife's personal use (she was also under indictment). She was a sitting Chicago alderman, and she was her husband's full-time campaign manager at the time of the crimes. News of the investigation by the feds broke, and Mr. Jackson sought immediate refuge for a mental disorder. He did not return to his office from that point on for several months prior to the general election in November of 2012. He made *no* (zero) public appearances during the primary or the general election. Surprise, surprise the Honorable Mr. Jackson was reelected in a three-way race. He garnered 63 percent against a white Republican (23.5 percent) and a black independent (13.5 percent). This is what drives people, who are not black, crazy. Not only did he violate his public trust, he had been carrying on an extramarital affair with a blond bombshell of a Latina in Washington for some time, and in fact this is what got him tripped up. He coerced a campaign contributor to pay her travel expenses because he did not want to pay for them himself. Lastly, this same shining light of a congressman had been involved up to his eyeballs in trying to buy President Obama's former Illinois senate seat. Regardless of all of this baggage, he got reelected and then almost immediately he and his wife copped pleas from the federal government. He agreed to resign his office as part of a plea agreement that also required an admission in open court that he had diverted at least $750,000 to personal use, and $600,000 of that amount constituted unreported taxable income (funny how that mental disorder claim vanished). What a swell guy! His run for reelection and subsequent resignation cheated his constituents of a fairly elected new congressman and allowed the Illinois Democrat governor to fill the vacant seat in concert with the Democratic machine in Illinois. Are black people served by these machinations of raw political power? No apologies from his father, the reverend, for this abuse of power and theft from the constituents.

In case you think these are simply aberrations, look at the same state for one Derrick Smith, a member of the Illinois House of Representatives who was booted from that body by a vote of one hundred to six for a bribery conviction. He ran for reelection in the Democratic primary and received 76.7 percent of the vote and cruised to reelection in the general election in November of 2012. Are you kidding me? Black people died and gave their hearts and souls for freedom and the ability to vote. Did anyone foresee these kinds of abuse and insults to all Americans? By the way, Illinois is currently financially bankrupt and one of the most corrupt states in the country. Should anyone be surprised?

These scenarios have been ongoing for decades from lower-level officeholders to mayors to US Congressmen and US Senators. I make no case for corrupt officials of any race, but for those who need positive representation most, the judgments in black communities to vote color rather than performance serves to continue their inequities into the future. It is akin to the people in Massachusetts who elect anyone with the Kennedy name regardless of their real qualifications or character. By the way, Charlie Rangel just won the Democratic primary in his district by a slim margin and will certainly be elected to another term at the age of eighty-four with all his baggage!

Chapter 11:

Who Is My Father?

One of the single most significant factors in black poverty is the number of children born out of wedlock to black women (the latest federal statistics show a 76 percent rate for children out of wedlock to black mothers, and this figure does not include abortion statistics for black women). It is not a matter of bad luck, predestination, impact of slavery, or current white subjugation. Rather, it has become a cultural phenomenon from the very poor to the very rich. Black men, it seems, have become grossly derelict in their treatment of women and particularly the children they have created. I readily stipulate that poor lower socioeconomic white males are in the same boat. There are now several generations of welfare mothers who have continued on the same path as that of their mothers and grandmothers in having children that they can't afford. The fathers use every means available to avoid any financial or emotional responsibility for their children. Many professional black athletes and celebrities making millions of dollars have to be taken to court and even jailed to be forced to pay court-ordered child support.

Rae Carruth, a wide receiver for the Carolina Panthers of the National Football League (NFL), had his girlfriend, Cherica Adams, killed so that he could avoid having to pay child support. Now that is up there for the all-time low. Yes, that was his motive for such a heinous crime. On November 16, 1999, his hired killers shot and killed her while she was eight months pregnant. He had money, fame, and comfort yet he thought so little of mother and child that he wanted them dead (this was almost four years to the day after the Million Man March on Washington). There was no hue and cry from the Jackson/Sharpton types who claim to represent the black community.

Does anyone remember the Million Man March of October 16, 1995? It was put together with the blessings of almost every civil rights group in America, and the Nation of Islam was a major player with the minister Louis Farrakhan being a prominent speaker at the rally. The goal of the march was to get black men from all over the United States to come to Washington, D.C., to take an oath to become better fathers, brothers, sons, and spouses. This obviously presupposes that things were not well up to that point. I believe that it is fair to say that more than nineteen years later the change has become nonexistent and by some standards worsened. Black women on that important day were urged to stay at home to demonstrate their concern over the abuses of their men. It was called the Day of Absence. The day was obviously very controversial given Farrakhan's significant role, but the biggest argument was over how many actually attended. The National Park Service, a nonpartisan source, came up with 400,000 (Bill Clinton was president at the time). The organizers claimed 837,000. Then ABC News funded a Boston University study that found the number to be 837,000 plus or minus 20 percent (thank you), either 1,004,400 or 669,600. What a joke!

So what has happened since? Drug abuse is rampant, black men are going to jail every day, women are as impoverished as ever, and black illegitimacy is epidemic. If anyone took into account black aborted fetuses, it would be even more staggering. There is a black man, Desmond Hatchett, from Knoxville, Tennessee, who has been adjudged to have fathered twenty-four children with eleven different mothers. He cannot pay child support. So who pays? You do. Warren Sapp, the former NFL football star and current NFLTV channel personality was behind in his child-support payments to the tune of $728,000, yet he was still on a national broadcast cable channel. Mr. Sapp (seems an appropriate name for this guy) has made $82,185,056 during his NFL career. He had $826.04 in his bank account when he filed for bankruptcy, and his NFL Channel salary is reported to be $540,000 per year. These types of stories are everywhere, and yet few are condemned as villains.

I do not make the claim that all or most black men are this sort of scum. I propose that Sodom and Gomorrah are not far away if the irresponsible in the black community are not shunned rather than celebrated. The real victims are always the children of such unions. White people are not superior in this area, but their numbers aren't in the same ballpark. There are deadbeats of every stripe in American society, but the problem is that when black people claim to start with such a disadvantage why wouldn't they be more circumspect? The simple reality is that victimization begets victimization, and until more thoughtful and serious black people speak out on the bums among them, the cycle of pain will continue ad infinitum.

What puzzles me most is that liberal women's organizations like NOW (the National Organization for Women, founded in 1966) stand almost silent on this major issue facing black and Latina women. Could that be due to their own backgrounds and insensitivity toward women of color? They certainly champion abortion on every level and encourage what many black ministers call black genocide. Children born in these circumstances are more likely to be poor, uneducated, or suffer from child abuse and jailed. The outcry should be deafening, but it is barely addressed in the national media.

Chapter 12:

Jackie and Malcolm

In my opinion the two most relevant black people in the black human rights struggle from 1950 to the present were Jackie Robinson and Malcolm X. Remember, this is only my opinion. I understand that Dr. Martin Luther King Jr. was a prominent figure in civil rights, but the two that I've cited made black citizens proud to be black, while Doctor King's efforts were to get equal rights for his race. Jackie and Malcolm had very similar character traits in spite of very different political positions. Both were bright, courageous, articulate, passionate, and solid fathers and spouses. They had unquestioned integrity and their legacies will endure forever.

Jack Roosevelt Robinson was born to sharecropper parents in Georgia on January 31, 1919. His father left their home when Jackie was only one, and his mother moved the family to Pasadena, California shortly thereafter. She worked very hard at a variety of jobs to support a family of six, with Jackie being the youngest. They grew up poor in a relatively affluent community like Pasadena (the home of the Rose Bowl).

Jackie was educated in public schools, and he excelled as a four-sport athlete. He later matriculated to Pasadena Junior College where he lettered in football, baseball, basketball, and track. He was a catcher/shortstop in baseball, the quarterback on the football team, and a guard in basketball (all leadership positions). Beyond his athletic prowess, he was a good student and popular classmate. It must be noted that, although there may have been some racial intolerance in Pasadena, he played with and befriended white teammates as well as classmates. He was not subjected to the same level of oppression and abuse as black people in the South.

Upon graduation, Jackie moved on to UCLA and continued his successes (becoming the first black athlete to letter in all four sports), and he added tennis to his sports portfolio as well. He was one of only four black members on the football team, and one of his black teammates, Woody Strode, later became a well-known and successful Hollywood movie actor. Ironically, he was least proficient in baseball of all the sports that he played at the time. In the spring of 1941, just a few months short of graduation, he chose to leave UCLA to go to work. That same senior year he met the love of his life Rachael "Rae" Isun, a student in the university's nursing program.

Jackie tried to play semipro football for a while, but World War II broke out, and he was drafted into the army in 1942. His first assignment was in a cavalry unit at Fort Riley, Kansas (yes, the same Fort Riley that I spoke of earlier). While there he met and was befriended by Joe Louis, the reigning world champion boxer, who was in a special services unit on that post. Jackie applied for and received an appointment to officer candidate school (OCS). He graduated from OCS in 1943 and soon became engaged to Rae. His first assignment as a second lieutenant was in a tank battalion at Fort Hood, Texas. He would soon be introduced to racial prejudice that he had not experienced before.

On July 6, 1944 he boarded a bus on the post with a fellow officer's wife. He was told by the driver to move to the back of the bus, and he refused to do so. The driver reported his refusal, and military police later arrested Jackie. He was questioned by an investigating officer who showed him no respect and demeaned him with racially baited questions. This same officer then recommended that his commanding officer refer him for a court martial, which he did not. Rather, Jackie was transferred to another battalion where that new commanding officer initiated court martial proceedings. Several charges were filed including public drunkenness (big problem since Jackie did not drink alcohol). By the time the court martial was to be convened in August of 1944 the charges had been reduced to two specifications of "insubordination during questioning." He was acquitted by a board of nine (all white) officers, and the army conveniently moved Jackie on to Fort Breckenridge, Kentucky where he served out his remaining time with a special services unit. He was honorably discharged in November of 1944 (the war didn't end until nine months later). This encounter with blatant racism showed the steely determination that would serve him well in the crucible that would be white Major League Baseball.

It was now early 1945, and Jackie was urged to play for the Kansas City Monarchs of the Negro Baseball League. He accepted an offer of $400 a month and thus began the most eventful baseball career of all time. That same year he was offered a tryout with the Boston Red Sox at Fenway Park. It was nothing but a sham to satisfy a critic of the team, who happened to be a Boston City Councilman. It should be noted that the Red Sox owner, Tom Yawkey, was a pure racist by any standard, and this franchise became the last to integrate in 1959. On October 23, 1945, Branch Rickey, the general manager of the Brooklyn Dodgers, signed Jackie to a professional baseball contract, the first such Major League Baseball contract for a black ballplayer since the 1880s, and the die was cast.

Jackie and Rae married on February 26, 1946. He was assigned to the Dodgers AAA franchise in Montreal, Quebec, Canada. The city was integrated and cosmopolitan, so there were no problems with the fans or residents there, but spring training in Daytona Beach, Florida, was a whole other matter. The club had to provide Jackie and his wife private accommodations with a black family because his teammates were staying in a whites-only hotel. There was friction with some team members, particularly those with Southern roots, but Mr. Rickey quickly brought that to a halt. Players on the Dodgers' Major League roster were also hostile to Jackie's presence for they knew that some of them might lose their jobs if Jackie proved to be successful. Once again, Mr. Rickey quelled that distraction with his new manager, Leo "The Lip" Durocher, taking charge.

Jackie was not near the best player in the Negro Leagues, but Mr. Rickey selected him because of his ability, character, background, and education. He knew that the man that he chose would face horrific pressure and racial attacks wherever they played and that this black man would have to have tremendous courage and the maturity not to fight back.

Most people know by now how this all turned out. His year in Montreal was beyond anyone's expectations. Jackie batted .359 with a fielding percentage of .985 and was named the MVP of the AAA International League. The following year, he moved up to the Dodgers and received Rookie of the Year honors from an all-white sportswriters' ballot. In 1949 Jackie was named the MVP of the National League in only his second year in the big leagues. He went on to play in six World Series with one World Championship in 1955 and would later become a first-ballot Hall of Famer.

The Dodgers owner, Walter O'Malley, decided to trade Jackie at the end of the 1956 season to their archrival the New York Giants. Jack's skills had been eroding due to a diabetic condition, and he retired from baseball shortly after the trade was announced.

There was life after baseball. He received an offer from the Chock Full of Nuts coffee company in New York City and became the vice president in charge of personnel. A black corporate executive position was unheard of in 1956 America. Jackie was thirty-eight years old when he retired, and he had a ten-year career. He continued his contributions to the civil rights struggle until his death on October 24, 1972, at the young age of 53.

Jackie's baseball achievements came a distant second to his actions as a man. His courage and class under intense scrutiny gave millions of his race a dignity that they had never experienced. The same year as his Major League debut, President Harry Truman had desegregated the entire United States military. In 1964 Jackie cofounded the first black owned commercial bank, the Freedom National Bank of Harlem, and in 1970 he established the Jackie Robinson Construction Company to build low-income housing for poor families. As a white man I marveled at this humble yet giant of a human being, and yet less than two decades after his death many athletes of color had little or no idea of who he was or what he had done for all of them. He came into baseball as a pariah and left with millions of baseball fans of all races and creeds loving him for the man he was and not the color of his skin. This was a tremendous breakthrough for all of us, but there was still a long way to go. Incidentally, a new movie *42* came out in 2013, and it was a better production of a 1950 movie *The Jackie Robinson Story* that starred Jackie himself (no small achievement) with Ruby Dee as his wife, Rae (Ms. Dee has been a cast member in many of Spike Lee's repertory film company's movies). He is now commemorated by Major League Baseball with a permanently retired number 42 for each Major League team (Mariano Rivera of the NY Yankees was the only remaining player to have that number on his uniform, and he has since retired).

Malcolm Little was born on May 19, 1925, in Omaha, Nebraska. He was the seventh of eight children by Earl Little, an outspoken Baptist lay minister and a follower of Marcus Garvey, the militant Jamaican, who was the first black man to espouse black separatism and the return of black people to Africa. This was obviously a dangerous stance for any Negro to promote in the 1920s, and this made his father a target for the Black Legion, understood to be the Ku Klux Klan of the North. Two of Earl's brothers had been killed by white violence with impunity. This did not deter preacher Little from his beliefs and actions. Earl moved his family to Lansing, Michigan, where his house was later burned to the ground by members of the Black Legion. He was ultimately killed by being pushed in front of a moving trolley car in 1929. His widow, Louise, was left to raise her children with little or no money available (a small life insurance policy was absorbed by the funeral). At the age of four, Malcolm was in a desperate situation along with his entire family when his mother was committed to a state hospital for depression. The children were separated and moved to separate foster care with white families.

Malcolm would ultimately become the greatest and most influential black spokesman (again, in my opinion) in the world. Here people may immediately challenge my position in favor of his famous contemporary, Doctor King, but I selected Malcolm for a very basic reason: his fight was to get his black brothers' and sisters' self-respect and not civil rights. His argument always remained the same: without human rights, civil rights became irrelevant. That single struggle goes on today almost fifty years after his death.

Malcolm Little saw the United States from ground level and, by his own admission, from the gutter. His family was dissolved by white government social workers, and after spending two years in white foster homes, he left school after the ninth grade and moved to Boston, Massachusetts, to rejoin his half-sister, Ella.

Shortly after arriving there, he learned to hustle on the streets and became somewhat self-supporting through various legitimate short-term jobs. His eyes and ears were always open for advancement into more lucrative criminal activities. He left Boston and moved to Harlem in New York City where he began a life of crime full-time, as a numbers runner, pimp, drug dealer, and some other forms of racketeering. By the age of twenty he was a full-fledged criminal known to police in the Harlem area, and he carried a gun. While in New York he ran afoul not of the law but of one of his criminal mentors who wanted to kill him over a numbers score.

A change of scenery was essential, and Malcolm left Harlem in haste for the more comfortable Boston locale again. He set up shop as a burglary gang's leader with two white women (one of whom was his full-time lover) and two other black men. Their specialty was burglarizing well-to-do white people's homes and fencing the stolen goods for cash to support their growing drug habits. This came to a crashing end when they were caught cold by the Boston Police. One of the black gang members escaped and was never seen or heard from again (looks like an informant may have been from within).

In February of 1946, all were found guilty at trial of breaking and entering. The white women received light sentences, but Malcolm and his close friend, Shorty, received maximum sentences of eight to ten years, each in the Massachusetts State Prison in Charlestown. Prison for black men has never been easy, but Malcolm was hostile to the world. He hated religion and its practitioners, he hated white people, and his guards were all white. He became a pariah even with other inmates, who nicknamed him Satan. He was on his way to becoming one of those convicts who would leave jail more dangerous than when they went in. A few years into his sentence, he began receiving letters from two brothers and a sister urging him to seek out the Honorable Elijah Muhammad, leader of the Nation of Islam. A short time after the letters from his family began, he tried sending a letter to Elijah Muhammad, and to his surprise it was immediately answered, and it encouraged him to seek enlightenment through Allah. The more he learned about the Nation of Islam, the more he accepted its teachings. They caused soul-searching in rewinding his life experiences and his personal failings. He became a voracious reader and was a sponge for knowledge. Malcolm would later claim that it was probably the best education he could ever get. He was being instructed by the master himself, and he accepted all that he was given with pure blind faith. In 1950 he adopted the new name of Malcolm X because he had learned that all last names of Negroes were slave-attributed names and that their ancestral names had been destroyed upon arrival in the United States. He was now a devout Muslim and a changed human being not recognizable from his past attitudes and actions. In August of 1952 he was paroled from prison and headed to Chicago to meet his savior, the Honorable Elijah Muhammad. Malcolm was personally tutored by Mr. Muhammad and soon was the Nation of Islam's primary recruiter, setting up temples all over the East Coast and into the Midwest.

For the next twelve years he became the spokesman for Elijah Muhammad to the world. He believed in all of the Nation's principles but was most recognized by white people as a black segregationist and white hater from publicly stating that *all* whites were devils incarnate. Unlike most black civil rights leaders of the time, he promoted fighting back against white tyranny and oppression. Most of all he called for black men to be self-respecting human beings no longer looking for scraps from the white man's table. I first became aware of the name Malcolm X from reading *Time Magazine* (I was an avid current events enthusiast). Time and all other national white publications treated him as a dangerous extremist. He and the Nation of Islam were marginalized as a tiny fringe group out of step with the integration philosophy promoted by groups like the NAACP (National Association for the Advancement of Colored People) and most black church leaders across the country. I mistakenly linked Malcolm with anarchists like Stokely Carmichael and H. Rap Brown as did most white people. The term black Muslims was mostly used to describe the members of the Nation of Islam, and this gave the sect a more sinister coloration, which was the intention of the white mass media of the times. Malcolm was fearless in his denunciation of white crimes against all people of color. He was a calm but fierce debater on the issue of race in America and always stood his ground against blacks favoring integration. The more his word spread, the more attention he received from the FBI, the CIA, and state and local law enforcement.

The first time I ever heard Malcolm was while I was a student at Boston College. He made an appearance on a local radio show with Jerry Williams, a legendary talk show host in Boston known for being direct, abrasive, and outspoken. I expected fireworks, but Jerry seemed interested rather than confrontational. The more that Malcolm spoke, the more he made sense. He made it clear that he hated all whites for their tacit approval or willing participation in their common treatment of blacks (not Negroes as they were then called by whites). He also took issue with his black brothers for their failure to unite and support each other as generations of white immigrants had done after arriving in America to face intolerance by the white establishment. He pointed out specifically Jews, Irish, and Italians. He made the case that without economic power, blacks could never overcome the stranglehold of their oppressors. He called on black people to eliminate tobacco, drugs, and stimulants from their lives and to be responsible sons, husbands, and fathers toward their women. I had never heard anyone address the race problem in such a direct and common-sense manor. This was not a love fest, and Jerry attacked him on the Nation of Islam's subordination of women as well as their attitude toward Jews in particular. Malcolm was never ruffled, and through it all he got his main message out for black people to unite, stand proud, and stop begging. This was the first time I had ever heard a black person so well-spoken and well-versed with facts. I told friends about my reflections, and they said that I had been conned and that it was well known that Jews (Jerry Williams was Jewish) were strong supporters of black causes and that I should wake up.

It was newsworthy when Malcolm broke with Elijah Muhammad in 1964, but I frankly paid little attention when it was reported that Malcolm had been suspended and ultimately broke with Elijah Muhammad.

I must be honest and tell you that Malcolm left my consciousness until the Spike Lee movie *Malcolm X* was released in 1992. I sat there in awe in the theater with my wife at my side. I couldn't believe how ignorant I had been to have not had enough intellectual curiosity to dig into the life and background of this incredible man. I have since read his autobiography as told to Alex Haley, the author of *Roots: The Saga of an American Family*. Malcolm's life story bounded off the pages, and he was really a simple man in so many ways. There was no pretense about him, and his goal upon leaving prison in 1952 was to serve his black brothers and sisters through Allah. He did this by his work ethic, his tenacity, his courage, and his integrity. There was no corruption in him, and under the magnifying glass, he was scandal-free. He faithfully served Elijah Muhammad until he found out for himself that the man who saved him was corrupt and the teachings he handed down as a prophet were not even those of the true Islam as spoken in the Quran from Allah. He traveled to Mecca as a Muslim pilgrim and experienced a true epiphany. He humbled himself before Allah and became for the first time a true follower in the guided path of Islam as a converted Sunni Muslim. He came away with a change of heart toward white people because he saw and learned that Islam was a religion for all people of all colors. He recognized that the spirit in the heart for other human beings was the true standard for all to be brothers. Malcolm had not retreated from his passion against the white establishment and their minions for their grievous sins and their ongoing mistreatment of all people of color. However, he could abide sincere and honest dialogue with those whom he could disagree with but still respect.

This newfound tolerance was troubling to both black leaders and white racists alike. He was changing the dynamic for philosophical discussion on civil rights to human rights for his people. He cared little about the Civil Rights Act of 1964 as a new beginning because he knew that this would not cause white people to treat blacks with any less contempt than since the black emancipation of one hundred years earlier. He stated openly that without black people knowing that they were the true *equal* of whites in all human endeavors that his black brothers and sisters would continue the status quo of inferiority. He was the fly in the ointment of the great 1964 party, and one must remember the chaos that has taken place over the last fifty years since: periodic race riots, the assassination of Doctor King, the drug epidemics in the black communities, police brutality, horrible educational opportunities, and the government's pandering for the black vote with no solutions in sight.

Malcolm's legacy is to have tried his very best to bring black people to a new place where they could be proud to be black and compete with whites on every level. He understood that political clout was critical. He constantly stated his disdain for so-called black representatives and liberals who had never delivered for the twenty-two million voters they purported to care about in the areas of education, fair and decent housing, and equal opportunity for all jobs. He stated openly that he would rather negotiate with people who were openly racist as in the South rather than Northern liberals who he said were never really trustworthy. Remember that upon John F. Kennedy's assassination he referred to it as "the chickens had come home to roost," implying that all of the United States actions against other nations had sown this act of violence. He was no fan of the Kennedy brothers (this is almost sacrilege in the world of black politics). Malcolm had prophesied that he and Doctor King would be assassinated within a few years at most, and it came to pass.

Malcolm X, the great recruiter, was the person most responsible for the conversion of Cassius Clay (before the first Sonny Liston fight) to the Nation of Islam. We should all know that after Malcolm's termination with Elijah Muhammad, Ali was used as a cash cow and he too ultimately left the Nation of Islam. Muhammad Ali went on to unbelievable heights and respect internationally because he proved himself to be the equal of any man. Like an idiot I gave seven to one on Liston in that first fight and lost twenty-one dollars trying to make three dollars, but I never bet against him again.

Malcolm and his family were constantly observed and harassed by the FBI (we now know the tactics employed against all-black groups under J. Edgar Hoover). Malcolm's split with Mr. Muhammad resulted in the Nation openly putting out a contract to kill Malcolm (there is little doubt today that the FBI was well aware of this and tacitly allowed it to happen). The Nation firebombed his house while his entire family was asleep and then accused Malcolm of starting the fire himself. He had refused police protection, and the police obliged him in spite of their own intelligence reports that he was going to be murdered. Do you think they wouldn't have protected a white figure of this stature from himself?

On February 21, 1965, Malcolm X was gunned down in front of his family while speaking to supporters in the Audubon Ballroom in New York City. I was ambivalent about this because I had no clue as to who Malcolm really was as did most of white America. Three people were charged and convicted of the massacre, and all were members of mosque number seven of the Nation of Islam. No one ever investigated fully, a possible conspiracy like with Doctor King. No surprise! He had been a thorn in America's side, and regardless of his importance in the black struggle for human rights, few white people cared. And now we have Louis Farrakhan as the leader of the Nation of Islam, and he throws gas on every fire he can to impede better race relations. He is truly hated by all white people that I know.

No one can ever know what would have happened if Malcolm had lived beyond age 39 but I know this, people of all colors listened when he spoke and I believe that he had turned a huge corner in his life when he entered true Islam. He had connected with leaders in Africa who universally supported his beliefs and he was treated as a statesman by the King of Saudi Arabia, Prince Faisal.

I have never been a fan of so-called Black Studies Programs, but the life stories of Jackie Robinson, Malcolm X, Dr. Martin Luther King Jr., and Muhammad Ali should be mandatory reading for *all* students in US History courses everywhere and soon. I understand the fight that would ensue, but they all bring such clarity to the issue of race. These two giants in the black struggle would be disheartened to see black America as it is today. As a white man, I and many of my fellow whites see more racial disharmony than ever before. There are many more opportunities for black people today, but the tone of victimization overwhelms any positive dialogue. Black men and women are positioned in every walk of life in this country, and their professional ranks are growing with each passing day. The sad reality is that rather than building on accomplishments and moving forward, the so-called black leadership continues to complain about the unfairness of society. It blames everyone but themselves for lousy education, drug-infested neighborhoods, black prisoner rates, little economic clout, and political disrespect.

The president of the United States, Barack Obama, was elected by many more white votes than black votes. Now into his second term, black unemployment is worse than when he took office, black youth unemployment is off the charts, the drug problems in inner cities are horrific, black-on-black crime is as bad as ever and black illegitimacy is higher than all other races. I do not blame these conditions on the president but on the black culture itself. I respect the words of Malcolm X and propose that unless and until young black children are conditioned to the needs for self-respect, educational achievement, a moral value system, and stable two-parent households, they will be doomed to the worst that society has to offer. It can be done, but it will not come from more money from "whitey" that is routinely siphoned off as it always has been.

Chapter 13:

The Oprahfication of America

There is another icon to offer as the antidote to the many sins of white people. What immediate thoughts does Oprah, that single name, conjure up? Some are power, persona, character, integrity, tenacity, soul, philanthropy, intelligence, fame, and cockeyed optimism. There are many others that could readily come to mind, but suffice it to say that she is one amazing woman. This one person has transformed the American dialogue. She transcends all boundaries of race, gender, politics, income level, and age. How could she possibly have managed to do it? She personifies single-mindedness and guts.

Oprah Winfrey was born January 29, 1954, to a teenage single mother in Kosciusko, Mississippi. Her name was actually spelled Orpah (from a biblical character), but it was so often mispronounced that Oprah stuck. She was left to be raised by her maternal grandmother when her mother moved on to Milwaukee, Wisconsin. Her grandmother imparted a value system that Oprah maintains today, and this was a big piece in her later successes. Oprah rejoined her mother in Milwaukee around age six and became part of a welfare-assisted family. Upon reuniting with her mom, she learned that she had a half-sister named Patricia (who later in life died from cocaine addiction). As if things hadn't been difficult enough, Oprah was raped by a family member at the tender age of nine, but she never divulged it until years later on her television talk show. She herself, became a single teenage mother at age fourteen, but her child died in infancy, and shortly thereafter she moved to Nashville, Tennessee, to live with her father, Vernon Winfrey. This provided her salvation for he encouraged her to do the best she could in school to be able to achieve her goals.

The odds were high that she would be a lost soul, but she found the inner strength to pursue an education, avoided the pitfalls of drugs that she had been exposed to, and worked very hard at her chosen career in radio while becoming educated. This did not square with today's race hustlers, who in 2014 still use slavery and white oppression as the crutch to accept failure for people of color. Malcolm X would have been proud of this lady's courage, human dignity, and pride in her heritage. She was no flash in the pan success. The odds against her were tremendous, but she became a woman of many firsts. She worked hard in high school and received a college scholarship to Tennessee State University, where she continued her part-time activity in radio. She was a sponge and learned how everything worked. After college she went into television full-time and embarked on her great adventure.

Oprah's first full-time job came as being the first black woman to anchor the evening news on a television station in Nashville. The rest, as they say, is history; this was one of many firsts to come with her wits, intelligence, compassion, and tenacity.

We all know of the success of her television show (the highest rated show on daytime television without a close second), but she is much more than a celebrity. Forbes magazine reported her wealth for 2010 at $2.7 billion dollars, attesting to her financial savvy.

Her other successes include writing five books, publishing her own magazine, having her own satellite radio channel (Oprah Radio), starting her own cable television channel (the Oxygen channel geared to women's concerns), and now she has her own network as well, OWN (Oprah Winfrey Network). Add to these an Academy Award nomination for her role in the highly acclaimed movie *The Color Purple*. Oprah's philanthropies are widely acclaimed. She is not only generous but hands-on with her projects to better people's lives worldwide.

She endorsed Senator Barack Obama for president almost immediately after his decision to run for president in 2007 but has constantly denied a rift since his reelection in 2012. She neither endorsed him nor campaigned for him in 2012.

The year 2013 brought out a side of Oprah that non-black fans had never seen before. She became embroiled in the Trayvon Martin case, of an unarmed black adolescent who was killed by a Hispanic neighborhood watchman named George Zimmerman. I will discuss what this has done to race relations in a later chapter. Ms. Winfrey equated the significance of Trayvon's death to that of Emmett Till whose torture and murder in 1955 in Money, Mississippi, was at the hands of two white men. Emmett was only fourteen years old and a native of Chicago. He was visiting relatives when he was alleged to have put his eyes on a white woman. These savages kidnapped him, unmercifully beat him, gouged out one of his eyes, and dumped his body in a river, weighted down by a cotton gin. A trial was held with an all-white jury, and in spite of overwhelming evidence of guilt, the jury returned with not-guilty verdicts after sixty-seven minutes of deliberation. This was one of many corrupt and heinous verdicts in the State of Mississippi even into the nineteen seventies. Oprah's hyperbole was a callous attempt at fanning the flames of racism when she clearly knew better. Ms. Winfrey also became embroiled in her allegation that while shopping in Switzerland she received poor treatment by a sales clerk and claimed that it was based on her race. The store investigated and found (after reviewing security tape) that nothing as alleged had taken place. She only recently has introduced race as the main factor for President Obama's problems with Obamacare (the Affordable Care Act). It has been clear since her early support of Barack Obama that he had become something special to her. However, when the President of the United States is determined to have *lied*, yes lied, continuously for three years about a significant portion of his healthcare plan, it matters not that he be white, black, or orange. The scorn of the electorate and the media is a reasonable expectation. I cannot comprehend how the most powerful woman in the country could stoop so low as to play the race card on these occasions.

I still respect and admire Oprah for her past good works and the model she has provided young black girls and women. I cannot pretend to know what she feels inside, but the events described above tarnish her icon status with fair-minded people of all races.

Chapter 14:

The Supremes to Gangster Rap

Music has always been one of the best uniting communication vehicles over the ages. Black people had no possessions when they were brought to this country as slaves. In spite of their torturous days, slaves had a common bond in music, and this ethic has continued to inspire them for decades. Emancipation did not equate to freedom in the deep South, but blacks could attend church on Sundays and enjoy religious hymns. They discovered their natural talents in singing and were able to use those to please pastors and other black folks. This heritage became fertile ground for gospel, blues, and jazz singers alike.

 The 1920s brought forth many black musical artists as well as bands. This era was the beginning for future stars like Ethel Waters, Bessie Smith, Ruth Etting, Louis "Satchmo" Armstrong, and Duke Ellington. They played to mostly black audiences and rose to the top of that clientele, and their songs are still played today. Black artists of future generations owed a great deal to such giants in the industry.

The 1930s were painful for blacks and whites alike because of the Great Depression, so music became a salve for the wounds of the spirit. Blues took hold, and musicians and singing artists filled a need in society at large. This period gave a national voice to the likes of the Ink Spots, Ella Fitzgerald, Lead Belly, Cab Calloway, Fats Waller, Lionel Hampton, Count Basie, Duke Ellington, Jelly Roll Morton, and the queen of soul, Billie Holiday. These stars faced racism throughout their careers but were undaunted in pursuing their artistic dreams.

Billie Holiday's music is still played today in various venues, and her songs did not have a color line. White people paid to see her perform in exclusive clubs even though she could not expect to mingle in that company. She led a somewhat tragic life with bad friends who introduced her to drugs and alcohol. She was at the top of the class during her career, but she disintegrated physically and died at the age of forty-four from cirrhosis of the liver. A tragic ending to a meteoric career.

A black giant of a man, Paul Robeson also rose to stardom during this period as a singer and actor, but more importantly he stood up for his human rights. He was the exact opposite of Billie Holiday. He was a graduate of Rutgers University as its valedictorian and had fame as a football player there. Mr. Robeson had a powerful voice, and he went on to success on the stage, in movies, and in song. His performance of "Ol' Man River" in the movie *Showboat* in 1935 is renowned for its passion and delivery. The world was at his feet when he consciously decided to openly speak out on the lack of equal rights for American black people and the rise of fascism in Europe. He became one of the first black targets of J. Edgar Hoover and his FBI. They smeared him at home and abroad to the degree that it affected his professional and private life. In the limelight of the McCarthy years, he testified before the House Un-American Activities Committee and stood up for his procommunist beliefs. Thereafter, his public career quickly faded, and he maintained his privacy through failing health. He died at the age of seventy-seven.

The war years brought on great black entertainers like Charlie "the Bird" Parker, Miles Davis, Dizzy Gillespie and Lionel Hampton. Nat King Cole was at the top of the pop music charts, gospel touring groups enjoyed sustained popularity, and the Mills Brothers produced hit after hit for all Americans to enjoy. The most powerful voice in gospel music was Mahalia Jackson.

The late forties and the fifties produced an outgrowth of rhythm and blues that became rock and roll, and the world of black music exploded. Young black men and women formed groups overnight and became sensations. One of the unanointed kings of the era was Chuck Berry, and he was enormously popular with the full diversity of the country. There were literally hundreds of black one-hit wonders as well as bona fide superstars like Jackie Wilson, Ray Charles, Sarah Vaughan, Sam Cooke, Little Anthony, Little Richard, Fats Domino, the Shirelles, the Angels, the Shangri-Las, Nancy Wilson, Dinah Washington, and Brook Benton.

In 1959 a black entrepreneur, Berry Gordy Jr. from Detroit, Michigan, started a company called Motown that revolutionized the black music industry. His stable began with Smokey Robinson and the Miracles and later included Martha and the Vandellas, the Marvelettes, Diana Ross and the Supremes, Stevie Wonder, the Temptations, the Jackson 5, and so many others.

The sixties also gave us the Queen of Soul Aretha Franklin, Marvin Gaye, Otis Redding, Wilson Pickett, James Brown, Jimi Hendrix, and composer Quincy Jones. This era also brought another black entertainer to a genre of music heretofore exclusive of *any* black people. His name was Charlie Pride, and he became a sensation in country music; yes, country music. Between 1969 and 1971, he had eight records that simultaneously reached number one on the US Country Hit Parade. Overall Charlie sold over seventy million records and received the top honors in the Country Music Association (Entertainer of the Year and Male Vocalist of the Year). He was inducted into the Country Music Hall of Fame and Museum in 2000. Can anyone imagine a higher mountain to climb in music? Remember that these are the same people that supposedly universally hate black people! There was no longer any racial bias in musical tastes.

The seventies introduced singers in bands like Sly and the Family Stone. Others like Gladys Knight and the Pips, the Jackson 5, the O'Jays, Roberta Flack, the Commodores, and Dionne Warwick enjoyed success with black and white audiences. Disco had its stars in Donna Summer and Barry White. Funk then came on the scene in the late seventies along with hip-hop, a type of street jive with rhythmic lyrics and rap. Black music was now popular across all color lines and grew exponentially.

Michael Jackson, the cute child that drew rave reviews with the Jackson 5 in the 1960s, became the musical genius of the eighties and nineties with his songs, music videos, and choreography. He became the first of many to become black megastars. Regardless of his apparent crossover to a strange sort of existence, he set a new standard for black success.

As an older soul, I still live in the fifties and sixties for my favorite choices in music, much to the dismay of my children as they grew up. I do know that I'm disgusted by the black and white merchants of death and destruction, who now prey on innocent youth with their horrible lyrics. They spew hate, disrespect, anti-social attitudes, racism and misogyny. It is a stain on so-called black leaders that they have allowed this so-called art form to spread more division between the races and foment even more abuse of young black women. The lyrics of a bygone era were about love and peace among all of us. We danced to these lyrics and had much more respect for each other than we do today, and that is a sad commentary for all races. People like Jay-Z and Kanye West are celebrated by black youth, the upper-class black folks, and even the President of the United States while being purveyors of the black culture's degeneration.

It is an interesting transformation that music that once helped tremendously in narrowing the chasm between the races is now serving to once again divide black and white people. I apologize if I have failed to mention some other great black artists, but I hope that the point has been made. The one-hit wonders all the way to the superstars of black artists have made a tremendous contribution to American culture. They are embraced by the vast majority of white people that they entertained.

Chapter 15:

Hollywood

Hollywood, the land where dreams come true, has not always been kind to black people going as far back as the silent movie days with D. W. Griffith's *The Birth of a Nation* in 1915. This film was a depiction of black people with all of the negative racial stereotypes. It presented Ku Klux Klansmen as a positive force for good (believe it or not, President Woodrow Wilson, a Democrat, thought the KKK was an appropriate counterbalance to reconstruction Northern carpetbaggers).

Movies have always been a great source of entertainment for white people, but it took up to the 1950s to portray black actors in legitimate roles as human beings. I have been a movie fan since my grandmother started taking me to the movies on Saturdays at the age of three. It became a weekly joy. I observed the transformation of African American actors and actresses (why are women now "actors"?) firsthand from stereotypical parts as butlers, maids, slaves, nannies, cooks, elevator operators, and the like. In spite of this, there were also spectacular specialty roles for dancers like Bill "Mr. Bojangles" Robinson, who danced with Shirley Temple and the famous Step Brothers who performed athletic and unmatched tap-dancing scenes.

Hollywood today is viewed as one of the most ultra-liberal cities in our country, but in the early days of the *big* studios and its moguls, it was strongly conservative. Black actors were largely window dressing for the film, but even in the 1940s blacks were rising above their expected station. People like Hattie McDaniel, who played the role of Scarlett O'Hara's nanny in the movie *Gone with the Wind*, received the Best Supporting Actress Academy Award for her performance. No small achievement for a film released in 1939 America. She had been no stranger to the silver screen, and she well deserved the award (this was seventy-four years ago). Lena Horne, the sensational black singer and actress, became the first black person to be signed to a long-term Hollywood movie contract. Later in the forties, the Disney movie *Song of the South* had James Baskett, an African American, starring in the role of Uncle Remus, a wise old black character from books in an earlier American period. It was of historical importance because it was Disney's first movie with live actors along with animated subjects as well. The movie produced the Academy Award's Best Song "Zip a Dee Doo Dah." It is the only Disney film not available in its original form today because black groups did not like the portrayal of the black people in the post-Civil War era as happy. The left has always had a strange sense of censorship when it suited them.

Hundreds of hardworking black character actors and bit players in comedies, dramas, and musicals toiled quietly at their profession. They were treated to the same discriminatory abuses when it came to accommodations, travel, and racial injustice, but they persevered in doing their best. There is very little mention of their stories in the civil rights struggle of the times.

The 1950s brought forward people like the gifted Dorothy Dandridge who was involved in the first biracial onscreen kissing scene in 1957 (this seems laughable now, but it was huge back then) and the smooth Sidney Poitier, who made ten movies during the decade with many being memorable performances, including his 1967 film *Guess Who's Coming to Dinner*, which put a face on interracial couples on a grand scale. He was the antithesis of black stereotyping. He was educated, suave, street smart, very good-looking, and brought great stage presence to most scenes. He could play any role with his range of skills as an actor, but most of all he had character and became loved by American and international audiences for his sixty-one years in films. His sole Academy Award came in 1964 for his performance in *Lilies of the Field*. He was a tremendous ambassador for people of color, and in fact he became the ambassador from the Bahamas to Japan in 1997.

The 1960s brought more black actors and actresses to the screen, but there was one black actor who hit his stride with significant roles in the following movies: *Sergeant Rutledge* in 1960, *Spartacus* in 1960, and *The Man Who Shot Liberty Valance* in 1962. His chiseled body and face, along with his stoic nature in films, were his trademarks. He had been an outstanding athlete at UCLA and shared the same football backfield with no less than Jackie Robinson in UCLA's outstanding season of 1939. Woody Strode made sixty-six films in a fifty-four-year film career. In 1967 alone Sidney Poitier starred in three additional epic films: *To Sir with Love*, In the *Heat of the Night*, and *Guess Who's Coming to Dinner* with Spencer Tracy and Katharine Hepburn (each movie dealt with race).

The year 1970 brought on a mixed bag of pluses and minuses for blacks in film. Blaxploitation films came on with Richard Roundtree in *Shaft*, and lookalikes followed with Jim Brown and Fred Williamson in similar roles. Melvin Van Peebles also came forward after years as a director, writer, and singer with *Sweetback's Baadassss Song* in 1978.

In 1973, two black actresses were nominated for Academy Awards for Best Actress. Diana Ross for *Lady Sings the Blues* and Cicely Tyson for *Sounder*. It brought credibility to the notion that black actresses could carry films given the right script and surrounding resources. Many have since been nominated, but only Halle Berry has won in 2001 for *Monster's Ball*. That, incidentally, was the same year that Denzel Washington won the Best Actor award for *Training Day*. One would think that two black people being so honored would indicate that there was a significant change taking place in Americans minds and hearts. It is odd that with all of the preaching that routinely comes out of Tinseltown, there would be such a dearth of Academy Award-winning African Americans!

The decade of the eighties signaled a dramatic change for blacks in the movie industry, thanks to a new superstar, Eddie Murphy Jr., and a dogged professional in film like Spike Lee.

Eddie moved from comedy stardom to film superstar. He was second in gross movie sales during his acting career, and he was extraordinarily successful in any movie genre he attempted (no Academy Award for him). He crossed all demographics of fan bases because of his comfort with all audiences. He is the master black entertainer.

Spike Lee, in my white mind, is a genius in film, but I have a hard time swallowing some of his personal antics. His release of erroneous information about Trayvon Martin's killer led to the infliction of serious pain and suffering for an entirely innocent white couple in Florida. He has demonstrated a very hostile attitude toward white people over his lifetime, and an *Esquire* magazine interview dating to October of 1992 gives evidence of this. Mr. Lee was unhappy with the result of that interview and has shopped for appropriate, deferring interviewers ever since. This having been said, I strongly disagree with the legions of white Spike Lee haters who infer that his movies spawn black racist attitudes. Anyone who has watched his contributions to the black/white dialogue in this country knows that he takes his black brethren's failings to task. His references to the history of white enslavement, torture, lynching, subjugation, retardation of educational opportunity, and general attitudinal racism are historical facts. His adoration of Malcolm X should give a good indication of where his heart is. He gave us the full Malcolm, the white-hating firebrand of his youth and early ministry for Elijah Muhammad, to the post-Mecca pilgrimage and epiphany of that same Malcolm with whom Mr. Lee seems to identify with in the end. I'll have more on Spike Lee later, but suffice it to say that this movie writer, director, producer, and sometime star has shown grit, determination and perseverance in pursuit of excellence in his presentations. His work is prolific, entertaining, and thoughtful and it will continue to stand the test of time (no Academy Award for any of his work to date).

From 1990 to present, black movies have moved to a darker side with few exceptions like Will Smith. The tone has less to do with current success stories than the notion of more and more white injustice through corporations and government. Remember, this is opinion based on my personal viewing and other interactions. I believe that there are thousands of heartwarming and inspiring movies to be made about black successes and black heroes and heroines. The problem is that these do not fit the culture of Hollywood. Drug movies sell, black women as prostitutes gets no hue and cry, schoolteachers in inner cities will not sell even though Blackboard Jungle, which starred Sidney Poitier, sold in the fifties. Not much has improved for people of color in inner-city schools sixty years later. Middle-class blacks are OK for television sitcoms but not for Hollywood. Yes, I am indicting Hollywood for its total failure to deal with hardworking, educated, dare I say religious, successful black men and women. The trash that it produces daily is amazing. It's no longer about storytelling with intelligence, wit, and style but about pandering to the lowest common denominator in our society. Our once proud culture has been debased to ashes. Now it's about special effects, the end of humankind, or a fantasy world for adults. Do you know how low a level we have sunk to? A first-class lady and star like Meryl Streep did a horrific hatchet job on Margaret Thatcher, the former Prime Minister of Great Britain, in a biopic probably written entirely by the British Labor Party. Are parts that tough to find that this world-class actress would need to do it, or is she just that liberal now? I hold out little hope for the future, but then again I was never a member of the Optimist Club.

I would be remiss in not saluting two of the greatest black actors to come to the stage and screen, James Earl Jones and Ossie Davis. These two men showed others how the craft should be performed. They have incredible biographies, and they always rose above racial obstacles placed in their paths. Their careers spanned more than fifty years with a hallmark of integrity, class, rectitude, and civility. Ossie in particular was a lifelong champion for civil rights. He talked the talk and walked the walk in his acting roles, playwriting, and directing of stage plays. He did not run from controversy but rather challenged the status quo in the treatment of people of color wherever he saw injustice. He was married to the same lady, Ruby Dee (a renowned actress in her own right), for fifty-seven years. Why aren't people of this stature celebrated and emulated in educational settings for black children?

Chapter 16:

Media Bias

Who is more unpopular than the US Congress today? If you were wise enough to guess the media in America, go to the head of the class. Nothing has changed American life over the past fifty years more than American television news organizations and the onset of cable television. The proverbial boob tube now dictates every aspect of our culture from sports to news to our societal well-being.

I had an interesting encounter one evening. I was expecting to meet two friends at the Waldorf Astoria Hotel in Naples, Florida, for a wine-tasting event at 6:00 p.m. I arrived at the hotel and asked where the event was being held and was referred to the concierge's desk for assistance. There was one person being attended to when I got there. He looked older, with white hair covered by a golf hat that kept his hair from rising. His clothes were less than sartorial; the black pants were baggy and not pressed or kept. The shoes were something from the old earth shoes out of the seventies recently removed from a Dumpster. I was astonished when I heard the person speak. I knew that voice, and as he turned slightly, I recognized that it was Phil Donahue. I was sort of dumbfounded by his very passive demeanor (maybe his appearance was an attempt at anonymity).

I grew up, so to speak, as a Donahue disciple in the sixties (I was still a registered Democrat back then). We came from very similar backgrounds, and I loved his daytime television talk show that originally emanated from Dayton, Ohio, every Monday through Friday. He was the first talk show host of a nationally syndicated television show to have any real success. His ability to get the most out of an interview catapulted him to fame and fortune. He was bright, articulate, charming, witty, and entertaining. His interview subjects were at the top of their professions whether it be politics, sports, the arts, Hollywood, science, or entertainment. All of his pluses had very little downside, but over time The Donahue Show morphed from apolitical talk to varying agendas and controversial subjects and guests. At some times it became the venue for any and all aberrant behavior in American society. I don't know what caused this, but it could have been about a chase for ratings since other talk show hosts were now everywhere on the television landscape. The other significant change resulted in Donahue's making it very clear to his long and faithful audience that he was a certified liberal voice on some of the most divisive issues of our time. I believe that he was right much more than he was wrong, but his antipathy to the Roman Catholic religion was visceral even though it had helped to shape him into who he had become. He would not stake out the position of an agnostic as I had with the same disagreements with the Church, but rather chose to flaunt his disgust with the Church's leaders and many of its tenets. This period well preceded the child-molestation crisis that later erupted within the Catholic priesthood.

I cite the above as a metaphor for where we have been over the past several decades and where we are now. Donahue was a star that rose from initiative, hard work, tenacity, and compassion. He lost his way, and rather than being celebrated for his many achievements, he is out in the wilderness and marginalized today by his fellow lefties. His demeanor onscreen became shrill, overbearing, and intolerant of views contrary to his own. Who could have ever expected Phil Donahue to have been ousted from MSNBC for not being liberal enough even though he led that network in their ratings at the time? Sure he is still a celebrity by today's standards, but who isn't?

Walter Cronkite is viewed by many in journalistic endeavors as the gold standard of broadcast news. I agree, and I never knew of his leanings to the left. He always separated his personal biases from the delivery of real news. Today there are no Cronkites but rather self-anointed interpreters of the news that gets presented to the public. The process is more about the production of so-called news rather than some of the airheads that read the product when the red light goes on during a broadcast (yes, I am discounting the intellectual prowess of the likes of Brian Williams). It is no longer what is important on that day but what the network deems to present as important. The movie *Network*, a 1976 production written by Paddy Chayefsky had been a precursor of what we are experiencing today. It was visionary and cynical about broadcast networks, and it could not have anticipated the impact of cable television. Anyone can look at that movie today and only shake their heads in its haunting parallels without having a clue as to how it came about. Many have theories on the causes: the Vietnam War, the loss of faith in our public institutions after Nixon, or the globalization of news interests. I have a simpler take on it. The lack of public awareness and self-education is the primary cause of our collectively being taken for a ride in a black limousine. Greed and lack of will to do the right thing on the part of the stewards of the Fourth Estate is a secondary contributor. The arrogance of the vast majority of reporters today on every level is demonstrated by their lack of human compassion for the effects of their sloppy and often erroneous reporting. Yes, this is an indictment of the entire system, and it matters not what network you watch. The driving forces are money and egos, and the trick is to become a celebrity rather than an honest journalist.

So what does this have to do with race? Everything. The news should always be about what is wrong or even outrageous by reporting it honestly and following up on the actions being taken to improve the condition. I propose that if the national news networks applied the same amount of coverage applied to the Vietnam War to the disintegration of public education for people of color, we wouldn't have had the chaos that exists today in public schools across America. Elimination of No Go Zones due to race would do wonders in the elimination or at least reduction of teen pregnancy among African American children that is at epidemic levels. A focus of legitimate scrutiny of black-on-black crime in urban areas throughout the country could serve to get politicians and law enforcement serious about the issue. A more aggressive approach to the malfeasance of black public officials like Jesse Jackson Jr. and his wife or Charlie Rangel could certainly help their constituents receive better representation. Simply put the main reason for the timidity to confront these issues with more resources and more reporting is simply the intimidation that comes from such work in the form of the *racist* tag. Let's take a look at these one at a time.

Try to imagine a week of news without reference to the president's campaign travels, or pick anything else regularly regurgitated and substitute in depth analysis of the New York City school budget, its drop-out rate, salary levels of *all* administrators including benefit costs, and the matriculation rate for black students to four-year and two-year colleges. This would be just scratching the surface. How about interviewing students adversely affected by grossly failing schools? What is the average cost per student in schools largely populated by African Americans and Hispanics? Have you ever seen such reporting on the evening news regardless of the network (after all, aren't all the really talented media people in New York City?)? I haven't. Black children were better educated in the 1940s, fifties, and sixties in segregated environments than they are today, and I challenge all the hand-wringing public school supporters including teachers' unions to deny it. The state and federal money that has poured into cities across the country for the supposed black students' benefit has systematically been siphoned off by bureaucrats, educrats, unions, and political cronies (this has been exposed by periodic commentary but without a follow-up).

There is a bottom line. Are black children even surviving public education? The critically acclaimed movie *Waiting for Superman* clearly stated that they aren't. Black children are now in a new form of slavery of the mind, and the plantations are their nonfunctioning schools. What's being done about it? More theory and more feel-good programs that have little to do with real education. Compare black education in America with third-world countries in our own hemisphere, and you'll be shocked how poorly we fare. Europeans and Asians take education quite seriously, while we only give lip service to it. Can anyone with half a brain not understand that the United States (as of 2012 rankings) is thirty-fifth in math, twenty-fourth in reading and comprehension, and twenty-sixth in science? Australia ranks seventeenth, twelfth, and sixth in the same respective categories, while Pacific Rim countries are at the top. We are on the RMS Titanic, and we're assembling the deck chairs in the event of an iceberg. We are in third-world status, and we don't have a clue!

There are no signs anywhere in newsrooms across this country that boldly state "Do Not Go Near Black Issues without a Black Reporter" or "Beware of Racist Charges If We Print This." We all know or should know that editors have these words branded in their brains. It is not about sensitivity but about cowardice in the face of facts. There are all kinds of acts of violence perpetrated by black gangs against white people, but these are rarely mentioned in print that this was a race-related or hate crime. Is that just an accident or by intention. I suggest the latter. There was a clear case of this nature in 2013 in Virginia Beach, Virginia, not long after the Trayvon Martin verdict. The local newspaper for whom one of the white victims worked would not publish details about the black assaults by as many as five black attackers that were known at the time. Who does this help? White people and black people are victims because the perpetrators feel they have license to act in the future in similar if not more violent ways.

This same blind eye is turned to black and Latino out-of-wedlock birthrates. Isn't it newsworthy that our inner cities are decaying brick by brick because of single mothers having multiple children without a supporting father? The statistics are brutal as to these children's incarceration rates, their drug use, their lack of education, and their propensity for violence. Is the goal in life having Michael Jordan basketball shoes or living an educated and healthy lifestyle?

Less than a year ago, the City of Chicago thought it was back in the Al Capone era with the daily violence and murders being waged by black gangs against its own black population. The death toll was warlike, and innocent bystanders were often the victims. National broadcasts particularly wanted nothing to do with the story. Remember, this is President Obama's hometown, the city's mayor, was Rahm Emanuel, President Obama's former Chief of Staff, and black luminaries like Jesse Jackson and the Rev. Jeremiah Wright were residents (although I assure you that their homes were safely out of harm's way, in much better environs). Yet none of this was deemed a significant part of the puzzle on national television and print media except for the Fox Channel. Yes, Fox was charged by many Democrats and black leaders as racist. Do you get my point yet?

Charlie Rangel should be in jail, and Jesse Jackson Jr. is in jail with his wife due to go in when he comes out (wouldn't this thoughtfulness by the US Justice Department be the same for a low-level drug-dealing couple?). These two are probably small fry when it comes to fraud and abuse of office. One only needs to look at the mayoral history in Detroit when it comes to a history of black corruption that has spanned decades without intervention. All of these mayors were black, and their victims were largely black. The city is in federal bankruptcy due to the mismanagement and malfeasance of almost entirely black-run administrations.

Casualties are without regard to race, and a once-spectacular city is on its knees. Any indictment of particular villains in the national media? That would be insensitive and surely have a racist bent. I and a significant number of white people ask but a few simple questions. Why do people of color so willingly accept such fates? Why do these same people allow themselves to be cheated of their earnings, accept terrible educations for their kids, and hold such low thresholds of success for themselves? Is this all Whitey's fault, or is a look in the mirror appropriate?

The media has a moral responsibility to black audiences to inform them of dangers just as they do for white people. The political part of media decisions as it relates to people of all colors should be trashed as a policy. I hold that reporters, producers, on-air news readers, editors, and media-outlet owners/shareholders be held accountable for the public trust they enjoy. Maybe Jesse and the ubiquitous Al Sharpton should organize a nationwide rally against the media's (they could call it the white media for better traction) complicit role with the cornerstones of black subjugation in America. Now that would amount to biting the hand that has fed them for over forty years. All of the horror stories mentioned were not suited for pieces on CBS's 60 Minutes or similar shows on other networks. There was no investigation on their parts prior to the fallouts. Do you think for one minute that this was by accident or these stories were really not worthy of coverage? Our Fourth Estate has not been asleep at the switch but rather they were part and parcel of the failures that have affected black citizens for the past forty years. Isn't it just a bit strange that Diane Sawyer could do a piece with the liberal view of affirmative action yet never be asked why there hasn't been a single black news anchor in the history of network news (pure and unadulterated hypocrisy)?

On a purely personal note, the inner-city black parents and children who do work hard at getting educated, who do have a moral compass, and who do not seek the supposed protection of a quota system are to be praised to the rooftops. They are what journalists should be seeking out for mirroring by their peers. Very few successful African American people have lived an obstacle-free existence. They have overcome by faith and tenacity against often incredible odds. Reporters in the quest for a Pulitzer Prize should examine closely how these people have achieved their goals. They do come from every background imaginable.

Chapter 17:

The Great Equalizer

Slaveholders in the South had a common rule for their slaves. *No education.* They knew that an educated black person would pose a danger to the slave system of grave injustice. Many of the leaders of slave revolts were either formally educated or self-educated. Education has long been the key to immigrant success in America. One need only look at recent strides by Asian populations in medicine, science, and engineering, and their appearance surely sets them apart from European white-bread types. These people, along with the Greeks, the Russians, the Italians, the Poles, the Slovaks, and dozens of other nationalities have faced the barriers of discrimination as well as the requirement to learn an entirely new and difficult language (English) when they came to America. So can we infer that the reason that black people cannot achieve is solely because of the legacy of slavery? This proposition begs the question. How have all of the successful black citizens of the United States managed to overcome this curse of slavery in their lives? The answer for most was their education, whether it was completing high school to be eligible for athletic scholarships or to simply aspire to become as good as they could be regardless of their supposed impediment. Every field of endeavor today has black people at the pinnacles of success. Look only to the current President of the United States, Barack Obama and the path he took to achieve his current status. Professional sports now have the white athlete in the minority, the art world is open and friendly to all types of artists, and the entertainment world may well be dominated by black men and women. Can you imagine that there are now black hockey stars in the National Hockey League? Chris Rock, the comedian, used to tell a joke about the terms "wealthy versus rich." His example was that Shaquille O'Neal, the basketball superstar, was rich but that the person who paid Shaquille his check for the Los Angeles Lakers was wealthy. Black people everywhere today are writing the checks now along with all other races and creeds.

The purpose of this chapter is to outline how negligent the so-called black leadership has been to have allowed the black educational experience to become so hollowed out and useless for urban black children.

We must first examine the historical view of black education.

- *1837.* The first black only university, African Institute, founded by a $10,000 contribution from a white Quaker philanthropist named Richard Humphreys, is now Cheyney University in Pennsylvania.

- *1854.* Ashmun Institute is the first institute for higher learning for young black men. Founded by John Miller Dickey and his wife, Sara, white Presbyterian Quakers. In 1866 the school was renamed Lincoln University (Pennsylvania) in honor of Abraham Lincoln.
- *1856.* Wilberforce University became the first black university to be owned and operated by African Americans through the auspices of the African Methodist Episcopal Church.
- *1869.* Howard University became the first black law school.
- *1876.* Meharry University opened the first medical school for African American students.
- *1881.* Spelman College was the first black women's college in the United States.
- *1881.* Booker T. Washington founds the Tuskegee Normal and Industrial Institute in Alabama for African Americans seeking higher academic learning with practical applications as part of the learning process. In 1896 George Washington Carver began teaching there and later achieved worldwide acclaim for his discoveries.
- *1922.* William Leo Hansberry, a white man, teaches the first course in African Civilization at Howard University.
- *1944.* Frederick Douglass Patterson founds the United Negro College Fund to assist African American children with college tuition assistance.
- *1954.* The historic lawsuit of Brown V. Board of Education of Topeka, Kansas. The US Supreme

Court rules that segregation in public schools is unconstitutional.
- **1957.** President Dwight D. Eisenhower, a Republican, orders the integration of the all-white Central High School in Little Rock, Arkansas. He federalized and ordered the Arkansas National Guard to return to their armories when Governor Orval Faubus, a Democrat, had used the troops to prevent black students from entering the school.
- **1960.** Black and white students organize the Student Nonviolent Coordinating Committee to combat segregation and discrimination.
- **1962.** James Meredith becomes the first black student to enroll at the University of Mississippi, one of many deep South universities hostile to integration.
- **1963.** The University of Alabama is integrated over the objections of Governor George C. Wallace, a Democrat.
- **1968.** San Francisco State University in California is the first four-year college to establish a Black Studies Program.
- **1969.** The Ford Foundation provides one million dollars to Morgan State University, Howard University, and Yale University to prepare faculty members to teach courses in African American Studies.
- **2003.** The US Supreme Court upholds the University of Michigan law school's student selection process with consideration for affirmative action.

- ***2007.*** The US Department of Education statistics reveal that in a survey of the top one hundred plus universities in America, the level of black faculty participation averaged 5.4 percent, less than half of the black percent of the population. The black percent of the US population for 2012 was 13.1 percent.

*** Thanks to "Infoplease" for this timeline.

This brief summary is instructive on several fronts. Before and after the Civil War, there were efforts on the part of white people to assist slaves and former slaves in receiving education. The black universities mentioned above are still stalwarts in delivering quality education to black children in this country. White philanthropists were genuinely concerned with the advancement of black people. The politics over the period covered were consistent. The segregationists were the backbone of the Democratic Party, while the abolitionists who strongly fought to oppose slavery were Republicans from the North. The post-Civil War South was routinely referred to as the "solid South" for Democrat public officeholders. The Jim Crow laws so often cited and referred to by our liberal friends today were enacted at the behest of the Democrat Southerners who had hated Republicans since Abraham Lincoln. Ku Klux Klan members have been prominent in Democratic Party circles for generations. A prime example was US Senator Robert Byrd (now deceased) from West Virginia. This "bird" joined the Klan at the age of twenty-four (certainly not a child) and rose to be the leader of his Klan chapter to boot. He refused to serve in the US military during World War II because he would be called upon to serve with (pick your most insulting name) Negroes. Then as late as 2001 he used the colorful but incendiary term "white nigger." Here's the problem. How many black or white people ever heard that the longest-ranking Democrat US senator had such baggage? Further, were they aware that he and many of his Democratic Party's senators, including Al Gore's father, tried everything humanly possible to kill the 1964 Voting Rights Act, which really served to truly emancipate African Americans? It simply amazes me that so many people of all colors have no idea of the real history of the political parties when it comes to race.

As a proposition, isn't it necessary to be literate in order to be able to learn academically? I suggest that it is. Black literacy rates from 1900 to present simply do not exist! There is plenty of anecdotal suggestion, but I don't care for that type of subjectivity. We spend billions of tax dollars now on the US Department of Education (thank you, Jimmy Carter) but try to get concrete numbers on this issue from them! The *Huffington Post*, a proudly liberal news source, reported on September 6, 2013, that there had been no measurable improvement in US literacy over the prior ten years. In 2003, 14 percent of adults were below the basic literacy level, and 29 percent were at the basic literacy level. As of 2013, 21 percent of adults were reading at below the fifth-grade level of comprehension! This is across all races, so if history holds true, the black experience is even more troubling. So what's wrong? Is it institutional racism, a lack of funding, a lack of enough black teachers, or a lack of understanding at the administrative level? All of the above? I submit that it has nothing to do with any of the above but rather a total lack of commitment to what has been demonstrated as successful.

The 1950s clearly had segregated schools for black children under the "separate but equal" terms mentioned earlier. The landmark ruling by the US Supreme Court that struck down this concept did little to change the well-entrenched notion of segregated schools all across the nation. The irony is that in spite of less funding, less-qualified teachers, less extracurricular activities, and less school-to-work opportunities, these black children could be expected to learn the basics of reading, writing, mathematics, and history. If one looks to 2014 (sixty-four years later), there clearly has been total regression in black education in the inner cities of America. Cities like New York had large black population centers like Harlem, which had a culture of its own. There were black businessmen, black professionals, black policemen, black entrepreneurs all working together with black churches thriving. Yes, there was crime and some violence in these communities, but nothing comparable to that being manifested today in every black urban area in this country. There were nuclear families along with extended families of aunts, uncles, and cousins as well. The road was in no way easy for these souls, but they had hope and aspirations that through education and hard work some success could be expected. This was the period from which the television show *Amos and Andy* was set against.

Let's take a look at a child of this period. Colin Luther Powell was born in Harlem in 1937 and later graduated from

Morris High School in the South Bronx in 1954. Look at his path to success sometime, and you will find that he faced the everyday obstacles of his race, but he overcame them through education and tenacity. He is but one of tens of thousands of black men and women of this period who proved that race could be conquered through education, good will, inspiration from God, and a supportive family consisting of a mother and a father. Is Mr. Powell revered by his own race? No. He was the first African American chairman of the joint chiefs of staff in the history of the United States military. He was the first African American national security adviser to President George W. Bush (also a first), and he became the first African American secretary of state. Wow. But is he extolled in his own black community? No because he simply worked for Republican administrations and therefore was only another Uncle Tom in the eyes of the black community at large. At the same time, drug kingpins, rappers with checkered if not disgusting pasts, and the likes of Jesse Jackson and Al Sharpton are stars to many black youths and embraced by the current African American president. It is beyond puzzling and frankly demoralizing to the average onlooker of black sentiments in 2015. The narrative of black victimization and oppression pandered to by the US media is disturbing. All the people in this country should find this oppression mentality to be counterproductive when so many black people (men and women) have succeeded through education, perseverance, and a work ethic.

In 2010 a documentary was produced to take a look at American public education in this country. The film *Waiting for Superman* was directed by Davis Guggenheim, produced by Lesley Chillcott, and narrated by Geoffrey Canada, an African American born in the Bronx, New York, all of whom had strong liberal credentials. They set about to determine reality versus long held excuses for the demise of black public education. They tackled the obvious question of "what goes on in classrooms" and came away with the clear conclusion that teachers were severely lacking in several areas: qualifications, discipline, methods of imparting curriculum needs, motivation, and strict adherence to teachers' union rules. They took serious issue with the role of teachers' unions' power in the reasonable administration of the troubled schools that they examined. Inept teachers could only be fired after herculean attempts to do so by building principals. Teacher unions routinely contested implementation of a new order to enhance better learning methods, and they were staunch defenders of the status quo regardless of the impact on innocent children. They fought charter schools tooth and nail and demeaned all of these alternatives as offensive to public education. (A charter school is a state-funded school that is funded at a per-pupil cost not to exceed that of a regular public school. They privately control hiring, firing, and all day-to-day issues. Most notably they are nonunion shops and therefore a direct threat to the coffers of teachers' unions. They, therefore, must be destroyed.) It was ironic that in some of the interviews that were part of the film, the most ardent haters of nonpublic options were themselves the products of private education.

The resources available to public schools were reviewed and found to be adequate by various analyses. There was significant misapplication of funds available to the classroom teacher and students because of bloated bureaucracies, support of union work rules and byzantine administrative hierarchies with varying levels of responsibility (the Tower of Babel comes to mind).

The new wave of testing created by the federal legislation referred to as "No Child Left Behind" was chastised by all educational participants as an obstruction to education. As an aside, our federal government cannot manage a one-person parade, so is it any wonder that the time, money, and effort wasted since its passage has produced literally no practical value. The disagreement comes when it is painfully obvious that public school teachers want *no* testing because they are all exceptional at what they do. The failing results are not attributable to them. The teachers interviewed complained about the "teaching to the test syndrome." Let's see: who would have to take the step to have students only taught to the test rather than take responsibility for the overall curriculum? You're right, it's the teacher. When questioned on this canard, the response was that the teacher is overwhelmed and *must* cheat to survive.

A major part of the film revolved around Michelle Rhee, the newly appointed (at the time) Chancellor of the Washington, D.C., public schools (reputed to be the worst public school district in America). I spoke of her in an earlier chapter, and she was portrayed as a crusader for reform with her sole mission of being concerned first and foremost with the delivery of quality education to *her* students. All other bureaucratic impediments were to be reviewed and dealt with on her terms. She had been given a free rein by a courageous mayor, Adrian Fenty. The movie described a whirlwind of energy, common sense, and guts. She was not out of the mold of upper-level school management but had been a classroom teacher. Her pedigree was Cornell undergraduate and Harvard master's degree (no dummy here). The documentary chronicled the immediate visceral hate from all unions in the system. Contrary to their routine proclamation about being about the kids, the union bosses knew that this was going to be about them and their perks. It was war from day one. There was little cooperation extended, but the Chancellor was fully armed for the public debate. She closed nonperforming schools with too few students to justify their existence. She went after the central office requisition process with a meat cleaver. She visited schools and met her students with the promise of a better future. The test scores appeared to be responding, and then *boom*, the mayor lost reelection (primarily on this issue), and her days were numbered. The most unfortunate situation in all of this was that the parents in D.C. showed little if any concern for their own children when they became the proverbial meat axe for the unions that had destroyed this system in the first place. I certainly sound antiunion, but the film independently came to the same conclusions.

The movie opened to critical acclaim and success, but take this to the bank: it has never appeared on network television, and it never will. It is too much at odds with the liberal education philosophy of more money, more money, and more money. There have been attacks since from the lefties in all quarters. I wonder aloud, can we examine the bottom line that the United States is heading to third-world status and the elitist public school supporters continue to promote the notion that we're OK with their stewardship? Where do the president's kids go to school? Here's a hint, it's not a public school or taxpayer-funded school! The same holds true for black members of the US Congress. Once again the underserved black community in Washington met the enemy, and it was them. Pogo would be proud.

Why am I so negative on public education? It is because every time someone mentions getting back to basics or doing things in education that have been proven to be successful in the past, the education lobbies howl things like Neanderthal, idiot, unsophisticated, and shortsighted. They entertain the notion that education is far too complex for those of us who have taught to comprehend. Go to any education conference, and I assure you that you will be underwhelmed by the discussion. I have never suffered fools well, and in my role as a school board member and chairman in an affluent community in New Hampshire, I had to be quiet and look to the end of the symposium for relief.

What are the biggest problems facing education in the twenty-first century?

- Reading instruction and comprehension must reverse course immediately.
- Return to core subjects for time application during the school day.
- Examine the disaster that is called Special Education.
- Refine ancillary courses to minimal time or elimination (these would be available in private after-school options).
- Eliminate the US Department of Education (no kidding).
- Restore discipline in classrooms for those who want to learn.
- Allow bright and even brilliant people to become teachers as they once were without the overbearing premise that teacher colleges and their curriculums produce the best teachers.
- Encourage homeschooling when appropriate rather than placing every impediment possible in its path.

As a product of the fifties, we were taught to read using the phonics method. That required sounding out letters to form words that had meaning. This had been the prime reading instruction tool for decades prior and since. Did some children encounter problems with this method? Yes indeed, but they were provided alternative instruction upon detection. Then came the revolutionary concept of whole language instruction brought forward by Ken Goodman in 1967. He was a professor of language reading and culture at the University of Arizona at the time of his theory (no kidding, that was his title). He became enamored with the linguistic opinions of Noah Chomsky, an avowed liberal and self-described anarcho-syndicalist (most would readily suspect pseudoscience here). Thus came the modern demise in reading skills in the public schools of America. A theory now supplanted decades of successful practice. This was only one of many such theoretical discoveries that have been shown to have failed miserably in the classrooms. The education elite in States and the federal government love to latch on to such ideas with failed track records because they abhor the simplicity of education by a qualified and dedicated teacher. New concepts and rules abound for endless teacher meetings and conferences. They incessantly want to reinvent the wheel. Reading comprehension testing was dismissed, and the reintroduction of phonics was fought by the impresarios of public education.

Rudolf Flesch, an Austrian-born naturalized citizen, wrote the famous book *Why Johnny Can't Read: And What You Can Do About It* in 1955. It took apart the look-say method of reading instruction. A 1985 report by a sponsored commission on reading by the US Dept. of Education was released under the title "Becoming a Nation of Readers."

Beyond all of the normal linguistic nonsense of such assessments, the overall conclusion was that teaching reading by phonics was endorsed as the more efficient and comprehensive method. So here we have a theory that supplanted established practice with disastrous results, and who pays? The children pay along with their parents. No private sector company here or abroad would adjust a production process without a pilot program with positive results well beyond their current experience. The education establishment in America takes the entirely opposite approach. So the net result is that reading instruction is turned upside down thanks to the ideas of two professors with no working knowledge of classroom applications (you can't make this stuff up).

The United States is far behind all other industrialized nations when it comes to actual time spent on classroom work. The school calendars are somewhat of a joke now in the Northeastern part of the country. Snow-absence days are made up in the month of June, which for all intents and purposes amounts to no education. The breakdown of the average school day with the noncore subjects included does not allow for proper work in the core areas of English (now referred to as language arts), mathematics, social studies, and science. Our priorities are out of focus. We are more interested in providing integrated arts, music, family sciences, health, and physical education at the expense of core knowledge and routine exercise. The subject of physical education amuses me because everyone knows that for decades now this element has been a joke. It has been about games rather than exercise, and obesity has been out of control for decades, so where's the purpose and effectiveness measured? I know that it will appear to be Dark Ages thinking but in our little grammar and high school there was no physical education, no art, no music, and no shop (these were all available to a degree in after-school programs). However, everyone learned how to read, write, add, subtract, multiply, and divide along with a solid sense of US history and science education. Now we have calculators available, cell phones, and smaller class sizes without a corresponding improvement in demonstrated proficiency. The Standard Achievement Test (SAT) scoring several years ago arbitrarily granted extra points to raise slumping annual SAT results. This is education in America.

Special Education was a good idea that has been allowed to run amuck by the federal government. It has been and is the fastest growing element of most school budgets today. While many school districts do their best to closely manage their budgets, they have no control over special education costs.

The noble intention of the law was to provide additional resources to children with defined medical problems to be educated in the least restrictive educational environment (normally understood to be an average classroom whenever possible). The reality today is general abuse of the program by selfish parents, a cottage industry of lawyers, and a built-in cadre of psychologists and psychiatrists whose prime incentive is to medicate children and qualify them as learning disabled. I witnessed this firsthand as a school board member for eight years as well as a parent and taxpayer. To make the point, there was a landmark case that came out of New Hampshire involving special education benefits for a child with an exposed brain stem from an injury. The child had no cognitive brain function and would never recover. The parents, through their attorney, sued the local school district under the law. The court held that the child qualified under the special education law, and monetary damages were awarded. How is that for Alice in Wonderland? Was that intended in the original legislation?

What are the cost drivers? A parent is not happy with their child's school because he or she is lazy or disruptive. They go to a special education specialty lawyer and demand a private school placement. The lawyer threatens a suit, and the school district caves on the advice of their counsel to avoid even higher costs in the matter. Bingo, the child now goes to a private school at taxpayer expense, and the proceedings are sealed from the public. Then you have children with severe learning disabilities whose parents wish to have their child in a regular classroom. This scenario requires a full-time special education qualified teacher along with additional paraprofessional staff member(s) to assist in the classroom (this is above and beyond the regularly assigned teachers charged with running the classroom for the other children). The dirty little secret in many cases is that severely disabled children with no, I repeat no, cognitive function are managed with these additional resources for the entire school day. My first year on the school board, I witnessed one such child at the elementary school graduation ceremony. I was amazed at what it cost the school district to make his parents feel that their child had somehow received an education. If you want to see a verbal brawl take place, simply have anyone bring such issues up at the town meeting or other budget review proceedings. It is truly a sacred cow, and like every well-intentioned government program, it is easy to be gamed by the unscrupulous out there, and I include parents in this indictment. Do you think black or Hispanic kids get these opportunities? Try again.

There are also separate transportation demands throughout the full calendar year as well regardless of parental availability or need.

Suburbanites should publish a handbook on how to work the system for inner-city families who get the bad end of the stick. I personally appeared before a US Senate committee to testify on the reauthorization of the law, and my sense was that few, if any, of the committee members had a clue about the various problems with the law. They smiled and listened, but there was almost no interaction with our panel.

The US Department of Education came into law on October 17, 1979, under President Jimmy Carter and a Democrat-controlled congress. It became operational on May 4, 1980, with a budget of 14 billion dollars. The department was culled out of the original Department of Health, Education, and Welfare to rise to a cabinet post with an expanded budget and autonomy. The 2014 budget has risen to 53.8 billion dollars, an increase of 284 percent in thirty-five years or an average annual increase of 8.1 percent.

Exactly what have we gained from this? You shouldn't be surprised when I say nothing and that it has been an absolute folly. Almost all educational yardsticks have gone the wrong way. We are less competitive internationally than we were in 1979, and we continue to fail to keep pace with our enemies in the world in mathematics and science. Taxpayers have sent their tax dollars to Washington with the hope of getting some of their own money sent back. Can anyone tell me how Arne Duncan, the current secretary, has made a difference? He has endorsed charter schools as viable instruments to correct failing schools. He has refused to push school choice as a means to provide inner-city kids the opportunity to be better educated. He sits in Washington, and for almost six years, he has witnessed the ongoing destruction of the District of Columbia school system that is entirely funded by federal money. Worse of all, he was superintendent of the Chicago School District before he came to Washington. I hate to be redundant, but are you kidding me? His predecessor, a Republican, brought forward the regulations for "No Child Left Behind," and how has that worked out? I find myself sounding very cynical, but where is the silver lining after thirty-five years? It would be funny were it not so tragic for the disadvantaged children in this country. I would have hoped that during the recent budget sequestration of funding a 10 percent cut in this department's staffing might have helped get people out of their own way, but no such luck. They enjoyed the same level of importance as our strategic defense.

Teachers have complained for years that it is nearly impossible to teach in classrooms distracted by abusive, threatening, and often violent behaviors by students who simply should not be there. The unions have done very little to address the well-being of their members and the improvement of classroom decorum. The movie *The Blackboard Jungle* from 1955 demonstrated the problem of chaotic urban classrooms, and it happened to co-star Sidney Poitier as an influential member of the class. Today we have administrators unable or unwilling to entertain legal action against juvenile miscreants for their removal. The passage of the Safe Schools Act required schools to report *all* incidents of violence or threats to police immediately, and school administrators still try to thwart this clear mandate. Police are unable to act if teachers and administrators are not there to file a complaint and move the offender to the courts. The courts, as we all now know, are very sensitive to the rights of criminals, but even they should not be constrained from punishing threats or acts of violence in a classroom for the greater good. The shield of Special Education protection in cases of violence against children, teachers, or staff should be eliminated. If necessary, an amendment to the law could expect the support of teachers' unions as well as the National School Boards Association. We kid ourselves when we try to believe that all children can be educated. The notion is utopian and hinders the proper conduct of educational pursuits.

There was a time in the 1950s and 1960s when very bright college graduates who had not initially thought of teaching as a vocation but later became interested could move into the classroom with little additional requirements. They were welcomed and given support to get their teaching credential with completion of a few courses. These men and women demonstrated skill and knowledge in their specialty fields that far exceeded their peers from teacher-preparation colleges. They were also put on a short leash if they could not adequately manage a classroom.

The scenario above is almost impossible today. A physics graduate from MIT (the Massachusetts Institute of Technology) has less of a chance of teaching in a public school than a graduate of a school of education at a state university. His credentials can be overwhelming based on three or four years of practical application of his knowledge and demeanor, but he will be forced to jump through hoop after hoop to meet the "standard" of a teachers' college graduate. So much for the best and brightest in education. As a point of reference, if you looked at the top twenty graduates of every high school in America, what percentage of these people would be looking to become a teacher? A relatively small number from my experience. The pay alone often discourages interest, never mind the subjects previously addressed in this chapter. Performance should always be the primary criteria for hiring and retaining teachers.

Another major problem in education directly attributable to union shops is the fact of life that last hired is the first fired during a reduction in force. The union stands unequivocally for seniority regardless of ability. A teacher can be over the hill, marking time to qualify for a pension. A second teacher can be performing all tasks exceptionally, volunteering for extracurricular jobs, bringing enthusiasm to every class, and getting the most out of the students. They both have exactly the same teaching positions. A reduction in force is announced by the school district. Who stays? The former for all the wrong reasons. In almost every occupation in private industry, performance dictates who goes and who stays. Guess what? The overall performance and productivity levels are higher when seniority is not the only factor to separation. Please do not tell me that there are no such dead-end teachers; they exist in every school in this country, and the students themselves can readily identify them. They are known to their peers as well, but who do they have to complain to? Their union representative, that's who. Fat chance of a positive outcome there.

Homeschooling is viewed generally by public educators as a sin against humanity. They would like to be able to punish such parents for the temerity to think that they are qualified to teach their own children. They never seemed to object to parents who teach their children to read very well before entering public school; in fact, they embrace it. The presumption is that such parents will screw their children up. The children will have poor social skills as a result.

These children will be less prepared to be competitive and meeting demands of standardized testing. These same educators have fought vigorously to deny homeschooled children the opportunity to participate in sports or other after-school extracurricular activities.

The evidence available to date denies all of the claims alleged by public school administrators and teachers. Homeschooling has been found to be a very positive learning experience that compares more favorably than public school educators continue to suggest. The canard that parents can't flunk their children is absurd because nobody seems to get end-of-year failing grades in public schools anymore, but I'd love to be enlightened. Homeschooled children are not locked in their homes. They have neighbors and friends like anyone else. They participate in club activities, sports, and social events at church or other gatherings. Their learning experience allows for remediation in the evening or the next day. Most state Departments of Education require reporting by the designated instructor as well as taking the same standardized tests that all other children must take. The strangest thing of all is that school districts pay nothing, zero for these children.

I know that this is anecdotal, but Tim Tebow is a pretty good ambassador for homeschooling as are his brothers. Why are these same complaints not leveled at young actors, actresses, or entertainers who have almost universally been taught by tutoring methods?

Finally, there is this most compelling indictment of public education for black inner-city children. The Marva Collins story first got my attention on a segment of CBS's *60 Minutes* program aired in 1979. Marva was a dedicated full-time substitute teacher for fourteen years in the Chicago, Illinois, School District. She left the school district, withdrew five thousand dollars from her pension fund, and in 1975 opened her own one-room schoolhouse in her home in Garfield Park, an impoverished section of Chicago. She named her school Westside Preparatory School and opened it with her two children and six other students in her first class. The other six black children had been labeled as learning disabled. The short version of her story is that she proved with unqualified success that these children could succeed, and the results were almost immediate. Her six outside students all graduated from elementary school, high school, and college to the accolades of many but to the consternation of educrats and the status quo. Her story was national news in magazines, television, and a 1981 movie appropriately titled *The Marva Collins Story*, which starred no less than Cicely Tyson and Morgan Freeman (he would later appear as Joe Clark, another believer in black student abilities, in the acclaimed movie *Lean on Me*). Remember that I have challenged the current Hollywood producers because these were films from 1981 and 1989.

Marva Collins ran her school for more than thirty years. In 1995, 60 *minutes* was openly challenged to return to Westside Prep to see that the Marva Collins story was a sham. These are the lengths that opponents of traditional education will go to disparage successes outside their ivory towers. To *60 Minutes'* credit, they did go back, and their original story of 1979 paled in comparison to the success demonstrated by interviews with the former students, all of whom were successful and adoring of their mentor.

The issue of school funding was put to shame as well. Marva, in her 2006 to 2007 academic year, charged $5,500 per student, while the city of Chicago's per student cost was more than double that amount. She proved that her methods of positive reinforcement, high expectations for student performance, safety, and an abiding belief that every black child can learn were in stark contrast to the failing public schools of Chicago (they are still failing black children today).

The saying goes that you can't make this stuff up. Why is there no public investment in schools like this? If you've read this far, the answer is simple. Too many adults have a stake in maintaining the status quo. Self-interest has always been a prime motivator; it's just too bad that black children in cities across America are being cheated and ignored regardless of the lip service of their so-called black leadership. What do you think Tavis Smiley from PBS would have to say about all of this from his Washington, D.C., perch?

Chapter 18:

The Power of Faith

We have moved from a religiously based country to a predominantly secular culture. The fact that you can introduce an article in Playboy magazine in a public school but dare not even mention the word *god* without being shut down or shouted down states the status of America in 2015. African American culture from the times of the slave trade included a strong religious component from African roots of religion as well as exposure to Christianity over time.

There were significant differences between Northern state African Americans and those of their brethren as slaves in the South. Free black people in the North were more prone to gravitate to independent black churches, while slaves in the South were proselytized by established protestant congregations of their masters. Slave owners preferred religious involvement for their slaves as a means of retaining better control (it was not altruistic). The net result was the assimilation of African Americans into the religious ethic of worship.

Let's fast-forward to the post-Civil War period. African Americans now had their own preachers, their own congregations, and their own religious freedom. The fact that they were still shackled by racism and punitive laws did not deter their faith. Their sense of religion gave them a moral code that whites had preached but not observed in their own lives. They were family oriented, knew right from wrong, and infused this into their children. Black churches were not only a place to worship, but also a venue to become better educated. Black congregations were a major source of mutual support in times of need, and ministers knew their members' needs spiritually as well as physically.

The notion of religious and moral responsibility served the black community well for decades. The late 1960s saw a significant white withdrawal from established religions: Protestant, Catholic, or Jewish.

Black congregations endured the same type of drop-off especially from younger people. The relevance of such institutions came under fire because the government became the replacement for the moral compass reinforced by preachers on Sundays. Middle-aged and elderly African Americans held on to their belief in God and their salvation, but they were dismissed by practitioners of "the church of what's happening now." Morality was a thing of the past. The new all-powerful interest was self-interest. You want money, steal it or get in the drug trade. You want freedom at sixteen or younger, get pregnant and the government will support you indefinitely. You want sex, it's there for the taking. You want control of a criminal enterprise, violence and killing are options.

I in no way blame African American churches or their ministers. I blame the people who have chosen to worship the golden calf of Moses's time. All of the whining about slavery, oppression, and racism ring quite hollow when young black people make choices that disgust their own elders, never mind disapproving white people. To make the point, do you think it's only white people who fear the young black man on the street who is dressed like a gangster with all of the accoutrements especially at night or in a known dangerous neighborhood? Let's get serious; the jails are overflowing with such young black men. The Nation of Islam has a long-standing history of working with prisoners to show them a better way. What is their success rate? Theirs is a religious and practical method of saving souls. It is a version of the dogma of Islam, and I dare say that even the Minister Farrakhan has to be dejected over the godless nature of young African Americans today (the same applies to young white people as well).

There is no visible sense of leadership that calls for a new day for African Americans. It would require eschewing immorality, such as sex without real love or protection against pregnancy and sexually transmitted diseases. It would declare a million abortions a tragedy for the black community regardless of what Planned Parenthood has to say. Real leaders would demand a voucher system for education to break the stranglehold of teachers' unions over their children's education (imagine if the Congressional Black Caucus took this as a mandate). Ministers should call for the National Guard to be used to protect African American lives when black-on-black bloodletting occurs, as recently seen in Chicago. A real leader does not tolerate inappropriate or criminal behavior whether it is from a rock star, a politician, an athlete, an entertainer, or a regular citizen.

I may be a cockeyed optimist (believe me, I am not by nature), but I believe in my heart that the grassroots of black America can be mobilized to affect a better future for their race. To do so, they have to send a clear message to their political representatives that they've had enough. A start would be to look within for legitimate solutions rather than holding their hands out for federal or state aid that maintains the status quo. I think of a man like Jim Brown who has worked tirelessly for his black brothers and sisters for decades. He has more guts and intelligence than any African American member of congress, and he has to be depressed when he looks over the black American landscape today. I would be shocked to hear him say that things aren't worse today than when he started his efforts to raise the human dignity of his people. I apologize for being redundant, but there are successes every day that we never hear about in all walks of life, but the hardcore unemployed are not victims of Wall Street but rather their own false prophets. The role of African American church leaders must be to educate, educate, and educate. A significant element in recovery from drug or alcohol abuse is the recognition of a "higher power." It is about time for missionary work in all of our troubled inner cities because each day now produces more and more casualties.

Chapter 19:

Hope and Change

This phrase coined by the 2007 Obama for President Campaign struck a nerve with the American public. There was hope that greedy and corrupt financiers and equally corrupt government officials had not destroyed our economy forever and thus our way of life. Change was to signify an end to the way government was being run for rich lobbyists at the expense of the shrinking middle-class working families and the poor. George W. Bush had run our ship of state onto the shore at full steam ahead, and for this he deserves eternal blame and scorn.

Barack Obama was a freshly elected US Senator from Illinois who portrayed himself as Lincolnesque in his being a champion of the people when he decided to run for the Democratic Party's nomination for president. He had no real record of legislative or leadership experience, and this was deemed OK with the voting public. His prime opponent from the get-go was Hillary Clinton, the supposed heir apparent for Democrats in 2008. It looked at the outset as a David versus Goliath matchup.

Hillary who would rip anyone's heart out to get her way was faced with a serious problem. Others in the field were of little concern, but attacking Obama posed the real risk of alienating a significant part of the party's base if she were not careful. She first dismissed him as a nice man who lacked gravitas in world and national issues. It was like a patronizing tap on the head to a child by an adult. This strategy didn't work. Obama stayed right on her heels and ultimately became her only clear opponent in the race. She tried two new shifts:

- The first was to engage the black voting block by speaking in black congregation services and pressing the flesh. She even took to blatantly pandering by mimicking old black dialect. This minstrel show shtick wore thin on her audience.
- She also sent her minions like former vice presidential candidate Geraldine Ferraro to take on Obama on the issues of the day. This was immediately castigated by the media as a racist ploy, and the campaign was over.

Hillary never recovered when the media that she had courted so well for years gave her the back of their hand. The lesson to be learned was to not attack Obama on issues because you were a racist if you did so. Some may say that this notion is ridiculous, but unless media outlets changed their slobbering affection for this black man, the game was his.

The general election was easier than Barack Obama's Democratic Primary fight. His opponent, Senator John McCain, was almost handpicked by the liberal establishment media. He was viewed by most voters as old, weak, and dangerous. His campaign staff took note of Hillary's earlier demise and was determined to avoid any possible charge of racism. They fought under the Marquess of Queensberry Rules (the original first codified rules of professional boxing), while the Obama people used street-fighting tactics and took no prisoners. The election was a clear knockout for Barack Obama who now became President Obama.

The only dissenting note in this coronation of the first black president came from the upstart Fox Cable Channel. They tried to point out several critical areas for public concern: his lack of experience on a world stage, his associations with known anarchists, his strongly liberal voting record, and his ties to a white-hating black theology minister for more than twenty years. Nothing mattered, and Fox became labeled as racist by almost every other media outlet (it continues to this day regardless of the validity of any issue raised by Fox), and the Obama Administration at one time put out that the Fox News Network was not a news organization. What do you think Richard Nixon thought of CBS, NBC and ABC?

So now we are six years into the Obama presidency, and how has the messiah of African Americans fared? Quite poorly if you look at the record with any objectivity. African American unemployment is and has been at record high levels for his entire term. African American youth unemployment is out of control. Education of the black populace has regressed by any performance-measurement standard. The "African American out of wedlock" birthrate is at 76 percent. Poverty in the black communities is at levels not seen since the Great Depression. Government spending is through the roof, but it hasn't translated to a safer, better-educated, and better environment for African Americans under this hope and change leadership.

Let's look at President Barack Obama's signature achievement, the Affordable Healthcare Act. It was passed entirely by Democrats in the House of Representatives and Senate with whatever this president wanted. The president sold the program by lying, yes lying, to the American people (black and white) about its most significant feature, keeping the choice of your doctor or hospital. This fact has now been readily conceded by his most ardent supporters. Now we have the recent revelation by one of the architects of selling the Affordable Care Act, Dr. Jonathan Gruber, an economics professor at MIT, that the basic premise for the financial stability of this act was to raise costs for the vast majority in order to transfer those funds for those without medical insurance. It is now 2015, and this legislation has been and continues to be an unequivocal job killer. The mandates of the law have reduced the once sacred forty-hour workweek to thirty hours for those affected, and that translates to a loss of income. Part-time employment is now the largest growing element in the employment numbers. What has changed for poor African Americans in healthcare? Nothing because their coverage under Medicaid continues as it always has under a different name.

Here are a few other tidbits that should concern African American supporters. Africa, as well as other parts of the world, is suffering from ongoing extremist Muslim violence throughout the region, yet we dare not be critical. The Middle East is more chaotic than it's been in decades since this president's foreign policy has taken shape. Our relationship with Russia is headed to Cold War-type hysteria. We have placated the likes of North Korea, Pakistan, and Iran (now on the verge of becoming nuclear armed). We are ridiculed throughout the world by friend and enemy alike. We have managed to overthrow two dictators in Africa: Mubarak of Egypt and Gaddafi of Libya. How has that all worked out for us or those countries? This has been a foreign policy driven by rank amateurs. I was equally disgusted with the George W. Bush flunkies who got us into two wars and drained our blood and treasury. I truly had hoped that our new president could change our foreign policy to reward our friends but punish our enemies. No such luck!

On the domestic front we have the following scandals in this administration:

- The Justice Department's compromised gun-running program, code named "fast and furious" that led to the death of a US Border Patrol officer and hundreds of Mexican citizens.
- The IRS-targeted conservative political groups prior to the 2012 election. The head of the IRS has taken the Fifth Amendment against self-incrimination and has been held in contempt of congress. Yet the African American US attorney general, Eric Holder, will not prosecute this culpable white woman.
- The State Department's handling of the assassination of our Libyan Ambassador along with three other American defenders in Benghazi. Just try to

imagine if this had happened under George W. Bush what the media outcry would have been like.
- The incredibly amateur hour rollout of the Affordable Healthcare Act.
- The new Veterans Affairs problems whereby veterans have reportedly died while being put on "secret waiting lists" for treatment. It is not an isolated incident but rather a systemic failure and management issue where VA employees hid the facts to receive government bonuses.

How many more government agencies are there to be corrupted in the two years remaining? Remember that this was promised to be the most transparent administration in history. How about his anti-Wall Street rhetoric matched by a continuing love affair for their campaign bribery!

Here is the most striking problem that I have with this president's worship status by other African Americans. He has no relationship with the average black man. He is a creature of privilege raised by white grandparents when he was abandoned by his Marxist Muslim father and then his mother. He attended the finest schools in Hawaii and went on to great universities. He graduated from Harvard as a constitutional lawyer and has gone about shredding that constitution to suit his presidential goals. He lives large and rubs elbows with the rich and famous while decrying the 1 percent top earners in America. He and his wife vacation in over-the-top, lavish splendor at public expense (the first lady's trip to China with her mother and children is exhibit A). His fund-raising belies his campaign promise of reducing influence from the wealthiest among us. He demonstrates narcissism not seen since Richard Nixon. He utilizes his attorney general, Eric Holder, in much the same way as Nixon did with his hatchet man, Attorney General John Mitchell. This president has attacked the exceptionalism of America, he has pitted rich against poor and black against white, while he and his cronies have played ball with the Wall Street financiers that brought this country to its knees.

I did not vote for a president in 2008, but I had hopes for Barack Obama because I sincerely thought that just as Nixon opened up China (he was a notorious anticommunist), the new president could ameliorate racial politics in America. I was awfully wrong. African Americans deserve better and so does America.

Chapter 20:

Black Heroes and Villains

HEROES

These people are listed in no specific order. Their importance is equal in my mind in providing positive perspectives of African Americans.

Eddie "Rochester" Anderson, Actor

He was a very successful black actor well before he came upon his role with Jack Benny as his valet. He took a small part in a radio show on March 28, 1937, and turned it into a career that lasted twenty-eight years. He convinced the audience that he was always one step ahead of his boss, Jack Benny, and he was beloved with his color-blind fans. He brought wit, humor, and intelligence to his character, and this was exactly who he was in real life. In 1962 he was listed by *Ebony Magazine* as one of the one hundred wealthiest African Americans. He was known for his generosity and philanthropies that continue today. There was never a hint of scandal associated with this humble and thoughtful man.

Gen. Benjamin O. Davis Jr., Air Force Officer

A giant in the annals of the civil rights struggle on a practical level. He was the son of the first black general officer in the history of the United States military, Brigadier General Benjamin Oliver Davis.

Benjamin Davis Jr. sought and received an appointment to the US Military Academy at West Point, New York, in 1932 after attending the University of Chicago. He was shunned by his classmates for his entire four years as a cadet and was only spoken to by white cadets in the line of duty. He had no roommate, ate meals by himself, and was treated as a nonperson. Most would have cracked emotionally, but young Mr. Davis used these methods to galvanize his determination to graduate. His 1936 yearbook *The Howitzer* cited the following from his classmates: "The courage, tenacity, and intelligence with which he conquered a problem incomparably more difficult than plebe year won for him the sincere admiration of his classmates, and his single-minded determination to continue in his chosen career cannot fail to inspire respect wherever fortune may lead him." He graduated in 1936, thirty-fifth in his class of 248 cadets. He was the first African American graduate from West Point since Charles Young in 1889. He and his father were the only two commissioned officers in the entire US Army when he was commissioned as a second lieutenant.

This was a hollow victory on his part as far as the army was concerned. He could not even enter an officer's club on post or expect to command a single white person. He was ultimately assigned to teach military tactics at Tuskegee Institute in Alabama as an officer at Fort Benning, Georgia. However, this turned out to be a game breaker for him because in 1941 the Roosevelt administration (under pressure to create more black units) opted to initiate a flight-training program in the Tuskegee area. Now Captain Davis was assigned as its leader at the Tuskegee Airfield. The whole operation consisted of entirely African American personnel from the cooks to the pilots, and Captain Davis was their appointed leader but most often he was their inspirational commander.

The Tuskegee Airmen ("Red Tails" because of their brightly painted aircraft tails) have now become famous from books and movies that detailed their heroism under fire. They overcame bigotry of the worst kind in Alabama, they were subjected to racist commanders above Ben Davis who tried to make their lives as miserable as possible, and they convinced an extremely skeptical War Department to allow them to fight in the European Theater of the war. They distinguished themselves as fighter escort pilots covering bomber runs into and out of Germany and more than proved their equal to white aviators in similar roles.

It is truly hard to imagine what Benjamin Davis and his men had to go through to be able to serve their country in a time of peril. A total of 955 pilots were trained through the Tuskegee Program from 1941 to 1946, and of these there were 355 deployed overseas. Eighty pilots lost their lives and thirty-two became prisoners of war.

These brave souls, along with their commander, returned after the war to face a loss of freedom that they had tasted in Europe. They were back to being treated as second-class citizens in spite of their overwhelming commitment and sacrifice. Ben Davis chose to stay in the Army Air Force (soon to become the US Air Force) and continued to make his mark as a leader (remember no affirmative action here but open hostility). He served this country for thirty-four years and retired with the rank of lieutenant general (three stars). In 1998 President Bill Clinton honored General Davis with the status of general of the air force (four stars) while he was on the retired list.

I would submit that few African Americans have been taught in school or elsewhere of the significance that this man had on the civil rights struggle. He led by example and courage, something sorely lacking from today's self-appointed African American leaders. He has made us *all* proud.

Dr. Martin Luther King Jr., Civil Rights Leader

There is the world of black people before Doctor King, and then there is the world after. He had roots in Boston as well as his home in Atlanta because he earned his doctorate degree from Boston University.

Martin Luther King, Jr. was the son of a preacher and was humble throughout his life. It is still hard to believe that he was assassinated at the very young age of thirty-nine (the same age as Malcolm when he was assassinated). His mission was to bring forward the reality that African Americans were being repressed and oppressed solely for the color of their skin by the white establishment. The ministry he took on was to bring compassion, dignity, and understanding to the needs of black folks. His vision of a color-blind society was noble and in the truest sense of our sacred founding documents, the Declaration of Independence and the US Constitution.

Once his message of peaceful protest against the tyranny of racism gained traction, he became a threat to government. It was local, state, and federal government institutions that had routinely denied black citizens of their rights under natural law. Powerful forces became aligned against Doctor King and his followers, none more powerful than J. Edgar Hoover and his FBI. Mr. Hoover, who has now been outed as one of the worst human beings ever to hold a position of civil trust, made the personal and political destruction of MLK his prime focus. He applied inordinate resources to this task and violated laws he was sworn to uphold to that end.

The historic March on Washington on August 28, 1963, marked a demand by African Americans that the status quo on race was no longer acceptable. Doctor King's "I Have a Dream" speech electrified the crowd with its simplicity and call for human justice. I believe that this was his finest moment not as an orator but as a statesman.

The year 1965 brought serious conflict between MLK and then President Johnson over the Vietnam War. Doctor King's open opposition to the war was humiliating to LBJ because of his earlier efforts to get the Civil Rights Act of 1964 passed. Today we can recognize that one should not have anything to do with the other, but LBJ was not a man to feel scorned. Again I must point out that I was led to believe (by the government orchestrated disinformation campaign) that MLK was a communist, a womanizer, and a bad person. I and many others have found out the hard way how wrong we were.

On April 4, 1968, Doctor Martin Luther King Jr. was killed by an assassin's bullet. I have previously described the incendiary fallout of this act on black communities throughout the country. Now, as I said, I was not a fan by any means of MLK, but when the FBI caught the lone assassin, James Earl Ray, I immediately found it less than credible. You can call me a conspiracy theorist, but this did not pass the smell test. Here we had an escaped convict from Missouri who took time out while on the run to become informed of Doctor King's itinerary and lodging location, purchased and trotted around a high-powered rifle, secured multiple false passports and was captured in London, England. This was trotted out and swallowed by most of the American public. Are you kidding me? The FBI wanted King to go away, and they came up with this guy. I believe in my bones, as does the King family, that this may be the greatest hoax ever perpetrated without full discovery. In any crime investigation, motive usually implies a benefit of some kind to the perpetrator. Who stood to gain most by Doctor King's death? The KKK, James Earl Ray, Snoopy? The US government through its agent, J. Edgar Hoover, could count on a leadership vacuum in the quest for human rights.

Muhammad Ali, Professional Boxer

Ali is probably the most transcendent black figure in my lifetime. He came on the sports scene as a brash, boasting young fighter that was a lightning rod for most white people's racist venom. His antics were a shtick that he brought to a science in promoting his upcoming fights. His rise to fame came in 1964 when he was a decided underdog (seven to one to be exact) against the world heavyweight champion, Sonny Liston. To be clear, I wanted to see Liston beat him to a pulp and to humble him a little. Ali won and went on to become perhaps the most heralded boxer of all time.

Ali, the man, was not only a great athlete, but he had innate intelligence about events and circumstances rarely articulated by African American athletes. He could best the most supercilious white sports journalist of the time, Howard Cosell, often leaving him speechless. It was 1967 and the

Vietnam War was being escalated by President Johnson, and when Ali was drafted he refused to serve on the grounds of conscientious objector (he was a practicing member of the Nation of Islam). He was charged with a crime for his action and all hell broke loose. He was vilified universally in the white community but was also taken to task by some in black leadership positions as well. Boxing federations stripped him of his titles, and he lost four prime years in his career. The US Supreme Court, in an eight to none decision (Thurgood Marshall abstained), reversed the ruling in 1971 and Ali became an icon of the antiwar movement, but more importantly, in his own black community he had beaten "the man" at his own game.

The road to regaining his title was difficult but very memorable, given that the prime obstacle in his path was one "Smokin'" Joe Frazier. Their three battles are boxing classics. The crown jewel in his career came about in 1974 in the Rumble in the Jungle against the reigning champ, George Foreman, in Kinshasa, Zaire. Ali used his charm and wit to harness the support of the local people and was treated with godlike status. He beat a bigger and stronger fighter through sheer guile by using the now famous "rope a dope" strategy that tired Foreman out to the point of near exhaustion. Now the former Cassius Clay from a middle-class family in Louisville, Kentucky, had risen to a level of adulation that few African Americans had ever achieved. Ali became the most recognized person in the world. He met and had audiences with world leaders to discuss issues relating to "his people."

I came full circle along with most of the rest of the country in appreciating who this man really was. I was privileged to see all of his fights and his ultimate resurrection.

Rep. Shirley Chisholm, Politician

A pioneer in every sense of the word for African Americans and women. She ran successfully for a congressional seat from New York in 1968 with the slogan "Unbought and Unbossed." She was a founding member of The Black Congressional Congress and was an unflinching fighter for African American human rights and equal rights for women. She was once quoted as noting that she encountered far more hostility as a woman than a black person.

I came into contact with this lady in 1971 during her congressional visit to Fort Dix, New Jersey. I was involved in the preparation of her itinerary on post when I worked for the commanding general. I wound up being part of her official military escort group. I found her to be very knowledgeable on what training was all about and polite to us all even though she was the dignitary. Her visit was striking in that I didn't even know there was a black congresswoman in the US Congress at the time (I had stopped reading *Time Magazine* because of their leftist slant on the war).

Much to my further surprise Mrs. Chisholm decided to do the unthinkable in 1972. She decided to run for her Democratic Party's nomination for president. She was openly opposed to the Vietnam War and had been from the outset. She had no real chance of winning, but she persevered to the convention.

George Wallace, the governor of Alabama, had been a candidate for the Democratic Party nomination as well until he was shot and paralyzed by an attempted assassination. Mrs. Chisholm took the time to visit Governor Wallace while he was hospitalized and was severely criticized by black leaders for doing so. It mattered not because she felt it was the Christian thing to do for someone shot like that. She stands in stark contrast with the current crop of women, and particularly African American women, serving in congress today. She had integrity, guts, and worked positively to get things done and left public service in 1982.

Tony Brown, Journalist

Mr. Brown had his own nationally syndicated television show in the early 1980s. I caught it by accident while flipping channels and became hooked from that time on. He was a strong proponent of a better education for black children and economic empowerment. He spoke of things that were antithetical to the demands of black leadership of the times (more money, more money, more money, etc.). He promoted that essential to any possibility of equal human dignity had to start with a good education. He put the onus on parents to do whatever it took to provide that critical element. The other essential ingredient was the need for African Americans to support their own people in business. He was certain that just as other groups that had come to this country united in their ethnicity to support each other African Americans should do the same. In 1985 he founded the Council for the Economic Development of Black Americans whose motto was "Buy Freedom."

Thirty years later, what's changed? Things have gotten much worse in the African American communities, and they will continue to worsen without serious attention to Mr. Brown's counsel.

Thomas Sowell, Economist and Philosopher

He experienced hardships throughout his childhood (his father died before his birth) and was one of five children. He was forced to drop out of high school at seventeen for financial reasons and issues at home. He was drafted into military service during the Korean War and wound up as a US Marine. Sounds like he was headed for oblivion: black, no high school diploma, and no job prospects upon leaving the Marines.

He applied for and was hired as a civil servant in Washington, D.C., and attended night classes at nearby Howard University while earning his general equivalency degree. He then received admission to Harvard University based on his SAT (Scholastic Aptitude Test) scores and two strong recommendations from his professors at Howard University. He graduated magna cum laude in 1958 with a bachelor of arts degree in Economics. He then moved on to Columbia University where he received his master of arts degree in economics and then earned his doctorate degree from the prestigious University of Chicago in 1968 at the age of thirty-eight.

He has become one of the most unabashed critics of the notion that somehow African Americans continue to need subsidies and special status because of the generational impact of slavery. He despises the premise that African Americans cannot achieve their goals, as so many others have in much more difficult times in our history. Doctor Sowell is anathema to the race hustlers and hand-wringers from the National Association for the Advancement of Colored People (NAACP). He is the epitome of self-help, courage in the face of adversity, and thoughtful discourse. His writings continue to echo the theme that African Americans have been patronized for decades with supposed beneficial government programs that have only served to demean the human dignity of black people. One of his most salient quotes is "If you have always believed that everyone should play by the same rules and be judged by the same standards, that would have gotten you labeled a radical sixty years ago, a liberal thirty years ago, and a racist today." Thomas Sowell is someone to be celebrated and not scorned as he is by much of the so-called black leadership in America. He stands tall, erect, and uncompromising in an era of vacillation and whining.

On July 12, 2012, he wrote in his column "The civil rights movement in twentieth-century America attracted many people who put everything on the line for the sake of fighting against racial oppression. But the eventual success of that movement attracted opportunists and even turned some idealists into opportunists. Over the generations, black leaders have ranged from noble souls to shameless charlatans. After the success of the civil rights insurgency, the latter came into their own, gaining money, power, and fame by promoting social attitudes and actions that are counterproductive to the interests of those they lead."

Andrew Young, Civil Rights Leader

A disciple of Dr. Martin Luther King (he was present when Doctor King was assassinated), Ambassador Young was the son of a school teacher and a dentist. Therefore, he came from a position of privilege unlike most of my black heroes. He gave up this status and used his education to try to make things better for African American brothers and sisters through working for and with the poor. He faced threats of beatings or even death by trying to register black voters in Alabama and Georgia, and he believed in his mentor's call for nonviolent protest to correct injustice. Mr. Young became the strategist for Doctor King's civil rights campaigns in Birmingham, Alabama (1963), St. Augustine, Florida (1964),

Selma, Alabama (1965), and Atlanta, Georgia (1966). This man was no blushing rose when it came to race and politics.

Andrew Young successfully ran for the US House of Representatives from Georgia in 1972, 1974, and 1976. He served honorably throughout that tenure. In 1977, President Jimmy Carter appointed Congressman Young ambassador to the United Nations where he served with distinction until August 14, 1979, when he was asked to resign by President Carter over a clandestine meeting the ambassador had with the Palestinian Liberation Organization (PLO). This was contradictory to US policy at the time. It was a courageous step at the time, but once discovered it was roundly denounced in congress.

The year 1981 saw his candidacy and election as mayor of Atlanta. He brought all of his many skills to bear and secured $70 billion in new private investment for the city. Suffice it to say he helped Atlanta become the first world-class city in the formerly deep South.

Overall I am most impressed with his pragmatic approach to getting things done versus being wedded to ideology. He has shown candor and intellect throughout his public career. Anyone can disagree with his positions, but he is always a strong advocate with facts at his disposal in any debate.

Jim Brown, Athlete and Civil Rights Activist

James Nathaniel "Jim" Brown was born in Georgia but grew up in Manhasset, New York. He was a star in football and lacrosse at Syracuse University and later became a football legend with the Cleveland Browns of the National Football League (NFL). His hero status in this book is not due to his being the greatest running back in football history, which he certainly was, but because of his dogged determination in trying to make his fellow black people understand the simple laws of economics.

Mr. Brown has made it his life's mission to bring an economic sense of purpose to the forefront of the civil rights struggle. He believes in basic tenets to success in a capitalist environment: education or job training, pooling common resources, and the purchasing power of any group of citizens. Jim learned from his own experience that education is critical in competing in the world of ideas.

The fact that so many African American children choose not to get whatever education is available to them disturbs him. He has dealt with gang members whose functional illiteracy is a motivator in their violent attitudes toward society as well as other gangs. What else are they qualified to do? He founded education and job-training programs to assist the undereducated to gain life-management skills.

He has been a strong advocate for learning from the experiences of other ethnic groups that have come to this country. The recognition that so many other nationalities came to our shores with little or nothing only to face oppression from the establishment of the times seems to be lost on black leadership. These people (Jews, Italians, Slavs, Asians) never had it easy, but they were united in everything that they did. They bought only from like groups and economically supported each other while all moved forward by degrees. They worshipped and worked together to achieve common goals.

Jim Brown has now achieved elder statesman status, but he was not always viewed by white people positively. He was an educated, wealthy black man in a racist America. Press types and even otherwise thoughtful writers routinely described him as *angry* because his didn't suffer fools very well. Jim Brown was certainly an intimidating presence by his physique alone, but add intelligence to the equation, and you have conflict with the media of the time. He sought no counsel but his own, and he acted as he chose to with some fallout. His moral courage could never be questioned because he has always been there in supporting African American causes. He stood next to Muhammad Ali when he had his boxing title stripped for his refusal to be inducted during the Vietnam War. That was not a popular stance in 1967, and I strongly disagreed with them at the time.

Jason Whitlock, Sports Journalist

Jason is one of only a few current sports commentators (another being Stephen A. Smith) who will call out African American athletes for their misdeeds. He is color blind in a medium of ultrapolitical correctness and has paid the price for offending the sensitivities of his current employer, ESPN (the largest sports network in the world).

He is intelligent, articulate, and does his homework on any issue that he takes on. He has been taken to task for being openly critical of fellow sports journalists (a taboo in that industry) but remains unbowed. His talent has always overcome his detractors.

The Williams Sisters, Professional Tennis Players

Venus and Serena Williams revolutionized the game of tennis for women. They brought power and athleticism that was unmatched prior to their arrival on the pro tennis scene. They also were the lily white tennis crowd's worst nightmare. They were black in all that entailed.

Their father, Richard Williams, taught them how to play on the public tennis courts of Compton, California. He groomed them not only in tennis but in competition and life's challenges. They won at every level, and each became the number-one ranked tennis player in the world. They have each one every major tennis title in women's tennis. The bad news is that Richard liked to rub the bluebloods' noses in it so to speak. He came from a very poor background and is a self-avowed thief. So now he and his prodigies were at the top of the world tennis stage! He made it clear as did his girls that they were not going to be conventional champions. There was palpable resentment from tournament committees and media types.

The lid blew off during the Tennis Masters Series held at Indian Wells, California, in 2001. Venus withdrew from a semifinal match with Serena only minutes before the match, thus allowing Serena to move onto the final, which she won. The crowd booed Serena during the match and awards ceremony and then shouted racial epithets at Richard and his daughters while they exited the arena. Richard later commented, "The white people at Indian Wells, what they've been wanting to say all along to us finally came out: nigger, stay away from here, we don't want you here." They have never returned to that site, and it is perhaps the most famous boycott in modern tennis.

OK, so why are they on this list? Simply because they know who they are and don't take crap from anyone. Richard would be referred to as eccentric if he was white, but he was routinely characterized in the media as troublesome.

Magic Johnson, Basketball Star and Entrepreneur

Earvin "Magic" Johnson Jr. was raised in Lansing, Michigan, the son of two working parents, and he had six siblings. The work ethic of his parents set a pattern for his participation in sports and his life after professional basketball.

The accolades for his basketball achievements are well known but are not the basis for his selection here. He has overcome adversity in his life from being a victim of HIV. He discovered who his real friends were when he tried to return to the NBA. Magic always carried himself with character and dignity. He never whined or tried to make excuses for his conduct but tried to move on with the life ahead of him.

He has been a shareholder of his former team, the Los Angeles Lakers, had a brief stint as an NBA coach, hosted a television talk show, worked as a basketball commentator on television, and now is a minority owner of the Los Angeles Dodgers. He created a business venture, Magic Johnson Enterprises, that has an estimated worth of more than $700 million. It has as subsidiaries a promotional company, a national chain of movie theaters, and a movie production company. Magic brought businesses to the inner cities so that they could get the spin off economical boosts that Jim Brown had touted for decades. He is another clear example of how African Americans can overcome any negative circumstances by perseverance and tenacity.

Denzel Washington, Actor

Denzel's father was a Pentecostal reverend that worked two other jobs, and his mother was a beauty parlor owner. His parents broke up when he was fourteen, and his mom enrolled him into a military academy for his high school education. He credits that move with probably saving his life because many of his former friends wound up incarcerated. He went on to receive a bachelor of arts degree from Fordham University in Drama and Journalism.

He has worked at his craft as an actor and excelled with a wide variety of roles. His peers have honored him with two Academy Awards, the foreign film press has chosen him for Golden Globe Awards, and he has received the Tony Award for his work in Broadway productions.

Denzel Washington is without scandal and is a strong Christian voice. He has been the national spokesman for Boys and Girls Clubs of America since 1993 and has been a board member since 1995. He is an even greater class act than he has portrayed on screen.

Tiger Woods, Professional Golfer

Eldrick Tont "Tiger" Woods has been a phenomenon since he first appeared on the *Mike Douglas Show* at the age of three striking a golf ball. He is the most recognized golfer worldwide in the history of the game. His father, Earl, molded him into a steely, driven competitor who conquered everything and everyone in his path. Tiger was not only respected but also feared by most of his peers in a noncontact sport. It was made perfectly clear that his goal was always to win, and second place was treated as a failure.

He brought pride to African Americans because he was beating the hell out of white golfers at their own almost exclusive domain. On the other hand, he drew resentment from white people for a variety of reasons: his multimillion dollar Nike deal, his fist pump after a win, his red-shirt trademark on Sundays (the last day of tournaments), and his comment about not being able to play at restricted clubs (no blacks or Jews). His game could not be demeaned so his persona was. Through it all he stood tall and was a credit to his race (one of many per his own statement). Tiger created philanthropies to serve underprivileged black youth and was an overall good citizen. I remember going to the Bahamas for a company vacation and arriving at the golf course only to find young Bahamians doing the Tiger trick of balancing a golf ball on the bottom of a golf club. His impact was worldwide.

For all of the above, he was my hero, but he proved to have a much darker side, which will be discussed in the next section.

The Wayans Brothers, Comedians

Keenen and Damon Wayans did what no one dared to do since Amos and Andy in the 1950s. They created and starred in a television show on the Fox Cable Channel with plenty of humor for everyone, including black humor. On April 15, 1990, the show opened and demonstrated that an almost all-black cast could be irreverent with every group, race, or nationality (today that would be virtually impossible).

This was raw comedy on a cable network with much lower so-called viewer standards than network broadcasts. The first two seasons were very, very funny, but the liberties taken by the writers (Keenen and Damon) caused friction with Fox censors. Ultimately, Keenen had enough of the interference with his creativity and remained only as an executive producer. Damon left the show after the third season to pursue a successful acting career.

The cast included Jim Carrey and his introduction to US television, Jamie Foxx (who moved on to become a great actor), David Allen Grier (who continued on to a career as a comedian and actor), and Jennifer Lopez, a member of the Fly Girls Dance Group (who went on to tremendous success as an actress).

In Living Color broke a lot of taboos and people were the better for it. Its departure in 1994 signaled an end to wide-open humor (even on cable) in favor of politically correct comedy (an oxymoron). My thanks to Keenen and Damon for their contributions.

Condoleezza Rice, Political Scientist and Diplomat

Condoleezza grew up in Birmingham, Alabama, in the 1950s and went to school in the turbulent racially charged times of the 1960s in Jim Crow Alabama. Her mother was a school teacher, and her father was a guidance counselor and Presbyterian minister. The family moved to Denver, Colorado, in 1967 and Condi attended an all-girls Catholic high school and graduated at the age of sixteen. She then moved on to the University of Denver where she received her bachelor of arts degree in Political Science, cum laude. She was inducted into the Phi Beta Kappa Society at the age of nineteen. She earned her master's degree in Political Science at the University of Notre Dame and then received her doctorate degree in Political Science from the University of Denver.

She was a Democrat until 1982 and changed her voting registration to Republican after becoming disenchanted with the foreign policy initiatives of President Jimmy Carter. Ms. Rice also cited the fact that her father had not been allowed to register to vote as a Democrat in Alabama but was allowed to do so as a Republican.

She has held the following high positions in Republican administrations:

NATIONAL SECURITY ADVISER TO PRESIDENT GEORGE W. BUSH

Secretary of state for George W. Bush

She left government service in 2009 and returned to Stanford University as a political science professor where she had taught from 1987 to 1993 and then became university provost until her political career began.

This woman has been routinely maligned by the hatchet people on the left of the political spectrum for one basic reason—she worked in Republican administrations. She has always been direct and responsive to even basic harangues from Democrats in congress. She is brilliant and an accomplished musician who grew up in the worst of racist worlds in this country, but she overcame all obstacles through hard work, determination, and self-confidence. She is the absolute antithesis of how Democrats portray African American women in the twenty-first century.

Dr. Ben Carson, Writer, Columnist, and Retired Neurosurgeon

Doctor Carson grew up in Detroit, Michigan, the son of Sonya and Robert Solomon Carson, a Baptist minister. Both of his parents had grown up in rural Georgia. His parents divorced when he was eight years old, and he and his brother, Curtis, were raised by his mom. He attended public schools and later graduated from Yale University with a bachelor of science degree in Psychology. He then went on to the University of Michigan Medical School (not a bad pedigree).

Doctor Carson became a professor of neurosurgery, oncology, plastic surgery, and pediatrics, and he was the director of pediatric neurosurgery at Johns Hopkins Hospital in Baltimore, Maryland. In 1987 he led a seventy-member surgical team in successfully separating cojoined twins, the Blinker twins, who had been joined at the back of the head.

He has become the darling of conservative viewpoints since he retired and began writing and speaking out. He is a very thoughtful and articulate speaker on almost any issue. Given his background, he is less than sympathetic with African American demands for more and more benefits from the largesse of government. As a physician, Doctor Carson always based decision making on factual data available, and he sees a US government incapable of the same process. He is not a knee-jerk conservative but a rather pragmatic practitioner of the art of what is doable for the greater good.

Many Americans today worship at the altar of "I've got mine, so I don't care what happens." This man is more than comfortable financially, but he has a sense of urgency to try to do what he can to save Americans from themselves. This crusader (he meets the definition) is willing to debate his detractors for all to see and he understands that the left will attempt to savage him (as they have with all African Americans who oppose their agenda of more crippling federal programs). Dr. Ben Carson is a breath of fresh air, and I hope that he will get bigger and bigger platforms for his common sense approach to saving this country from the chaos, debt, and moral bankruptcy that exists today.

VILLAINS

Al Sharpton, Civil Rights Advocate

Let's start with the most recent news on brother Al. On November 19, 2014, CNN reported that Uncle Al owed taxes to local and state governments and the IRS in the amount of 4.5 million dollars. Maybe President Obama and his friend Eric Holder can give him another hug of support to make it all go away!

Al is universally the most hated black activist in America when it comes to the white viewpoint. I have not assigned his title of reverend because that like everything about him is fraudulent. He, more than any other single black man, is responsible for the steady deterioration of race relations. Orlando Patterson, an African American sociologist nailed it when he referred to Al as "a racial arsonist." Liberal African American columnist Derrick Z. Jackson has called him the racial equivalent of Richard Nixon and Pat Robertson (now that's high praise indeed).

Most people haven't a clue as to how Mr. Sharpton arrived to be the moral spokesman for people of color in America. It is a tribute to his main attribute as a hustler. He is accepted as a reverend while his entire history is anything but that of a man of God. There is no record of his attending, let alone graduating, from any theological or divinity school. He allegedly "preached" a sermon at the age of four, so he is assumed to be the Tiger Woods of theology! So the absurdity continues with his primary occupation having been the tour manager for James Brown, one of the great soul singers of my generation.

The basis for his ranking is that he is a first-class bigot who has made a living with race baiting at events devoid of racial animus. Al began his climb to notoriety in 1984 when he went after the subway vigilante Bernhard Goetz who shot four African American muggers who had no clue that he was armed. There was little if any pity even from black subway travelers for these miscreants with long criminal rap sheets. The federal investigation that he requested, along with other civil rights leaders alleging civil rights violations, was found without merit because the issue was about robbery and not race.

The Tawana Brawley case should have disqualified Al Sharpton from any future persona on behalf of anyone. The young lady, fifteen at the time, had been missing and then turned up days later covered with human feces and racial slurs written on her body. She alleged that she had been raped by two to six white men and one of them had a badge. Sharpton, Brawley, and her attorneys refused to cooperate with police or state prosecutors and openly alleged that one of the perpetrators was one Steven Pagones, a local prosecutor. The whole thing was a sham and had not of scintilla of truth to it. Brawley, Sharpton, and her lawyers were found guilty of defamation in a lawsuit by Pagones. Sharpton's share of the liability was $65,000 but he never paid a dime. Atty. Johnnie Cochrane of O. J. Simpson fame and other Sharpton supporters ultimately paid the judgment. Al never accepted responsibility and insisted he was guilty of nothing. Anyone surprised?

The Bensonhurst section of Brooklyn became the site of an incident in 1989 between a group of Italian men who were alleged to have attacked four innocent African American men, one of whom was shot and killed. Sharpton, only days after the killing, initiated marches to protest before the criminal investigation could get traction. He secured the agreement of the three victims to refuse to cooperate with law enforcement unless more black lawyers were hired by the prosecutor's office! He obstructed justice for his own agenda.

The great and powerful Sharpton interjected himself into the Crown Heights Riot in 1991. This was a case in which a Jewish driver in the Crown Heights section of

Brooklyn, which was heavily populated by Jewish residents, was involved in a car accident that resulted in the death of a Guyanese boy named Gavin Cato. It was a tragedy of errors with absolutely nothing to do with race, and yet Sharpton initiated more protests, and these led directly to the blatant public execution of a visiting Jewish student from Australia by a black mob with some chanting "kill the Jew." Any apologies from Al? No. And the sitting New York mayor, David Dinkins, an African American, tried to prevent the protest without cooperation from Al.

Al apparently had to improve his international affairs résumé so in 1991 he headed to Puerto Rico to protest US Navy target practice exercises and was arrested and served time (about three months) and went back about his business of race hustling.

The Duke men's lacrosse scandal of 2006 brought an almost immediate response from Al. The alleged victim of rape was an African American student at North Carolina Central University in another part of Durham, North Carolina, whose part-time employment was as a stripper/escort. Sharpton immediately found the poor woman credible, but if this was a reversal of racial participants, he certainly would have sung a different tune as he always had.

This case had it all: sex, race, an elite school, well-to-do white male privilege and a poor black woman. The problem was that it was all a horrific fabrication on the part of the victim. She wasn't raped by the accused or even physically abused. The rush to judgment against the Duke players was sweeping. The Duke administration imposed sanctions without even a hearing. The Duke faculty carried out what was the equivalent of lynching their own students (this from supposed liberal people). Media outlets had vitriol that was careless and misplaced. Civil rights groups were unabashed on the whole power dynamic of rich/poor and black/white even though it was not relevant in the end. A politically motivated prosecutor wove indictments from whole cloth and eventually was prosecuted and disbarred for his actions.

The whole episode proved that people were readily willing to accept the notion of white versus black power. It was immediately adjudged "a hate crime."

Apologies were deafeningly lacking from all quarters, and there was no condemnation of the perpetrator by so-called national civil rights activists.

Then heaven really shone on Al. On February 12, 2006, George Zimmerman, a community watch member, shot and killed a young African American, Trayvon Martin. This was what Al and his partner Jesse Jackson dreamed of. A perfect scenario with a white man (even though it turned out that he was uncomfortably Hispanic) and a poor unarmed innocent black victim on his way home. Sharpton used his old playbook, demanding an investigation beyond the one conducted by local police. This call was acted on by the Florida attorney general who overstepped her authority and turned the case into an unwinnable second-degree murder trial. Allegations that Zimmerman was a racist had no sustainability by local and FBI investigations. It turns out that Zimmerman was sympathetic toward African Americans and had in fact acted in their behalf. The forensic evidence with Zimmerman showing significant signs of being assaulted further mitigated against the second-degree charge.

The net result was that George Zimmerman was acquitted, and this produced another storm of racial invective by Sharpton and his allies. The only thing that produced a calming element was the call for peace by Trayvon's parents, who were exemplary throughout their ordeal. The irony was that those who wanted Zimmerman's blood the most created the atmosphere that eliminated the probability that Zimmerman would have been found guilty of the more appropriate charge of voluntary manslaughter. In their zeal, they compromised a reasonable investigation without political interference. No apologies from Al were forthcoming, only hyperbole over the verdict.

I apologize to you, the reader, for what might be perceived as rambling about this pariah of the African American populace, but few people can comprehend what a foul ball this guy is and how he has the attention and support of people who should know better. By the way, his net worth is estimated to be $5 million; is he one of the rich that he routinely assails?

Eric Holder, US Attorney General

Not since John Mitchell, President Richard Nixon's attorney general, have we had a more partisan and corrupt person in charge of the US Justice Department. He is the clear hatchet man for his president. His failure to be able to come up with any serious convictions from the Wall Street debacle is incredible when one considers how quickly he will go to federal court against states on states' rights issues. Mr. Holder has no interest in voting rights violations by New Black Panther Party members caught on tape. He has little curiosity when it comes to the Alcohol, Tobacco, and Firearms Department's (under the control of his Justice Department) allowing over two thousand assault weapons to get to the Mexican drug cartels. He is fighting tooth and nail against requiring a voter ID for voting (that country north of us, Canada, has had such a law for years) even though an ID is required for almost every activity in America. Mr. Holder prompted three federal denial of civil rights investigations involving Trayvon Martin, Michael Brown and Eric Garner. All were found to be WITHOUT MERIT.

I had a hope that Attorney General Holder would rise above race and prove that we are a nation of law. Instead he has demonstrated the attitude that his tenure is about payback against political enemies of his president. He has assured the white backlash that has taken place over his more than five years in office. He has been, without question, the most corrupt and partisan Attorney General of the United States since John Mitchell in the Nixon Administration.

Harry Belafonte, Singer, Actor, and Social Activist

Harold George "Harry" Belafonte was born on March 1, 1927, in Harlem, New York, to a housekeeper of Jamaican descent and a Martiniquan chef. He was sent to live with his maternal grandmother in Jamaica when he was five years old. He then returned to the United States in 1939 and attended public high school before dropping out and joining the US Navy during World War II.

After his military service, he held menial jobs until coincidence and fate brought him to a production at the American Negro Theater in New York City. He immediately fell in love with the possibility that someday he could become an actor. The costs for his acting lessons were covered by his freelancing as a singer in nightclubs, and that led him to folk music and his first recording contract. Harry was on his way. The 1950s brought success beyond his wildest dreams. Harry Belafonte was in demand as an accomplished actor and top of the charts singer.

The fifties also brought him into the civil rights struggle as a confidant to Dr. Martin Luther King Jr. There was discrimination everywhere, and Harry embraced the opportunity to lend his talents to fighting against such injustice. He championed humanitarian causes worldwide using his own money and auspices to try to make a difference in education, fighting AIDS and hunger.

Beginning in the 1980s Harry became more politically strident in his criticism of US foreign policy (he was certainly not alone on this). However, it became quite clear that his political bent was more comfortable with the ideals of communism and Marxism. His early political mentor was Paul Robeson, but Harry did not get shunned by Hollywood or the recording industry as did Mr. Robeson. There was now a zealotry and hostility to anything American, and it was fanned by those of the far left of the political spectrum. Harry traveled to Cuba and met Fidel Castro with whom he had not a single problem in spite of the chaotic conditions in that country.

The year 2002 marked the end to any pretense that Belafonte was other than a very angry and resentful soul. He took license with an earlier Malcolm X quote and said:

"There is an old saying, in the days of slavery. There were those slaves who lived on the plantation, and there were those slaves who lived in the house. You got the privilege of living in the house if you served the master, do exactly as the master intended you to serve him. That gave you privilege. Colin Powell is committed to come into the house of the master, as long as he would serve the master, according to the master's purpose. And when Colin Powell dares to suggest something other than what the master wants to hear, he will be turned out to pasture. And you don't hear much from those who live in the pasture."

This dismissed the entire narrative of who General Powell was and what he would later accomplish simply because he served his country all of his adult life.

Then in 2006, Harry and two other socialist cronies, Danny Glover and Dr. Cornel West, traveled to Venezuela to pay homage to their new hero, Hugo Chavez. Chavez just happened to be the new dictator extraordinaire out of the Castro playbook. The meeting produced the following quote from Harry:

"No matter what the greatest tyrant in the world, the greatest terrorist in the world, George W. Bush says, we're here to tell you: not hundreds, not thousands, but millions of American people support your revolution."

He had now been stripped of his cloak of sincerity and could be seen as an American hater of the first order. America was not the country that had made strides in civil rights, offered hope to *all* people who would risk death to come to its shores, or provided military and humanitarian support whenever it was needed. No, it was to be repudiated at all times. And for these antics, he is still a darling of the left.

President Obama, who now runs "the house" mentioned earlier in Belafonte's quote, has also been the target of verbal abuse from this "civil rights activist." It appears that the president is not liberal enough.

Dr. Cornel West, Philosopher, Academic, Activist, and Author

Here we have a legitimate African American intellectual with a spectacular academic pedigree. Dr. West was born in Tulsa, Oklahoma, and he was raised in Sacramento, California, along with his three siblings. His mother was a teacher, and his father was a defense contractor with the US Air Force (not much deprivation here). Young Cornel had a rebellious nature and was drawn, as a young man, to civil rights demonstrations and protests.

He received his bachelor's degree from Harvard University and his master's and doctorate degrees from Princeton University. He has been a professor at both of his alma maters and has had political conflicts at each of them resulting in his departure. His writings on race have a clearly socialist narrative. The good doctor would not be happy with America unless it embraced communism and opened a few gulags.

I have seen him on various television talk shows discussing racial flare-ups. His insight is predictable. It is the poor black person being oppressed by evil, capitalistic, and racist American society. He attributes little responsibility to a failure of black leadership, and he certainly knows better. I honestly know of no one I've seen that enjoys hearing himself speak more than Dr. West. He and his partner, Tavis Smiley, are the Batman and Robin of racial political theater. They have all of the solutions to the ills of our nation: monetary reparations for slavery, higher payments for welfare, housing availability for all regardless of ability to pay, higher paying jobs for all black people regardless of ability, free higher education and preferential admission standards, free cell phones, and a black President (oh, we have that). They're serious about these issues.

To demonstrate his bona fides as a socialist, he has attacked President Obama as a "war President with a peace prize" and "a black mascot of Wall Street oligarchs." It always strikes me as odd that these wealthy, ivory tower types always tell the downtrodden how bad the rich and powerful are, and yet they are rich themselves and have a voice that few white Americans have. Does Dr. West send the IRS more money (for the good of all) than his accountants chisel to the penny? What's your best guess?

Rep. Maxine Waters, Politician

A true practitioner of self-enriching oneself after election to public office. This woman, who brought new meaning to the loudmouth politician, became a multimillion-dollar citizen thanks to her South Central Los Angeles constituency (one of the poorest in California) and the rest of us. She like many others in her Democratic Party has had an abiding love for Fidel Castro.

She has served on the House Financial Services Committee and is now its ranking member. Therefore, the question must be asked where Maxine was during the subprime debacle? We know that it is a fact that she openly supported legislation for One United Bank while she and her husband had a significant financial interest in that bank. This is the same woman who is always screaming about how the rich abuse the poor.

The ultimate question of her real relevance is whether South Central Los Angeles is a safer, more prosperous, and better-educated community since her election to public office in 1976. I dare say it is not. Unfortunately she will continue to be elected by huge margins from people who don't know any better.

Group Award for Black Athletes with the Most Illegitimate Children

* Charles Rodgers—Former NFL player, five children with four women
* Larry Johnson—Former NBA player, five children with four women
* Marshall Faulk—Former NFL player, six children with at least four women (he has a steady on-air job with the NFL Network)
* Ray Lewis—Former NFL player, six children with multiple women (he has a steady on-air job with ESPN Sports Network and had baggage of being at least an accomplice to murder on his résumé)
* Antonio Cromartie—NFL player, seven children with multiple women in at least five different states
* Shawn Kemp—Former NBA player, seven children with six different women (recent reports allege as many as eleven children)
* Jason Caffey—Former NBA player, ten children with eight women
* Evander Holyfield—Former Boxing Champion, eight children with an untold number of women
* Travis Henry—Former NFL player, eleven children with ten women
* Calvin Murphy—Former NBA player, fourteen children with nine women

These are the tip of the iceberg when it comes to current African American athletes' proclivities to the same behaviors.

Orenthal James "O. J." Simpson, Retired NFL Superstar, TV Broadcaster, and Actor

Very few African Americans have fallen from grace as has this man while having the outrageous support of a black community that he wanted nothing to do with. I personally thought he was one of the finest running backs ever to play football. O. J. Simpson now stands for getting away with murder. For all of those African Americans that were rightfully outraged by the Trayvon Martin verdict, what did you think of the cheering crowds that reveled in the acquittal of a murderer who butchered his wife and an innocent man?

Those who thought this was finally a verdict on behalf of African Americans are surely concerned that the murderer of Nicole Brown and Ronald Goldman is still at large (remember that O. J. vowed to find the real murderer). There were so many things wrong with this case:

- Did O. J. look just a little bit guilty with his parade on a Los Angeles freeway with an army of the Los Angeles Police Department following him?
- Did the lack of sympathy for Nicole Brown, the mother of his children, have anything to do with her *race*?
- Were onlookers at all dismayed by the skill exercised by O. J.'s Dream Team of attorneys as opposed to prosecutor Christopher Darden's (an African American) famous asking Mr. Simpson to try on previously dried bloodstained gloves thus creating Johnnie Cochran's famous line, "if the gloves don't fit you must acquit."

- Did most African American O. J. worshippers have any clue that O. J. was more in tune with a white lifestyle than the vast majority of his blind supporters?

White people were universally upset with the acquittal but more so with the in-your-face attitudes displayed by African Americans in all quarters toward white Americans including the Brown and Goldman families. It was a clear image of what would come in the future, outright hostility to anyone white, with ridiculous rationales for the worst of attitudes.

O. J. in 2007 ultimately let his vanity get the best of him and sought, through criminal means, to recover some of his sports memorabilia, and as karma for his past horrific deed he will be in jail until he is a very old man. Any quibbles on the above qualify for psychiatric help.

Roland Martin, Journalist

This should be an honorable-mention award because I do not want to confer on him any sort of real status. Americans got to know Mr. Martin from his hiring by CNN as a political analyst.

It didn't really take very long for me to peg him as an African American bigot. His racial prism for every issue brought to a discussion made it very clear that he believed in white guilt for everything wrong in America. He was almost seething with venom when he attacked so-called white corporations or white politicians or whites accused of anything. His handlers seemed to really enjoy his antics, and he got more and more face time. Then, *boom*, he tweeted something perceived as antigay: wow, faster than a speeding bullet, CNN, the ultraliberal network, unloaded him. So here he got hung on his own biased petard. It couldn't happen to a nicer guy.

Mike Tyson, Boxing Champion

One strange dude. He, by his own admission, was headed to a life of crime with the expected result of death or incarceration when an old white guy named Cus saved him from himself.

Cus D'Amato had managed the boxing career of another African American champion, Floyd Patterson. He saw raw talent in Mike Tyson that Tyson didn't recognize in himself, and Cus took him into his home and trained him. He told Mike that he could be the youngest consolidated-belt boxing champion of all time if he did what he was told and shown. Mr. D'Amato not only made him into a fighting machine, but he also helped him in all areas of his life (Mike Tyson readily acknowledges this even today). Then on November 4, 1985, Cus D'Amato died and any chance that Mike Tyson would have a successful boxing career, financial stability, and a supportive family went out the window. He went on to win the three major boxing association championship belts by 1987 at the age of twenty, honoring his mentor as the youngest fighter to ever do that.

Enter the likes of one Don King, an African American boxing promoter extraordinaire, to oversee the dismantling of everything that had been working for Mike in the past. King robbed him of his money, his self-respect, and his manhood. The sordid nature of Tyson's moral bankruptcy, drug-addicted behavior, marital problems, and fighting decline fed a horrific image of him as a black lost soul. He was convicted of raping a young African American woman in Indiana and headed to a prison term in April of 1992, and his fighting career was put on hold.

Mike Tyson regained his championship title after he was released on probation in 1995 and then took on Evander Holyfield (who had come out of retirement) in a bout that Tyson was heavily favored to win. Uh-oh, Holyfield won on a technical knockout. Then in a rematch Mike Tyson did the unimaginable; he disgraced himself by twice biting Holyfield's ears during the fight, which ended the fight and sent Tyson to fighting oblivion.

He has reinvented himself as a movie actor and the star of his own one-man show on Broadway, a play titled "Tyson: The Undisputed Truth," a verbal autobiography. Spike Lee was the director, and the play was filmed and released as a movie. I watched, and my emotions ran from empathy to scorn, to laughter, to sympathy (when he described his absence when his daughter died), to amazement that he actually carried it off. The unfortunate reality is that he was given enormous opportunities, and he squandered most of them because of his own stupidity and callous disregard for everyone around him. He was a devastating puncher and bully who turned into a bum of the first order.

The real Tyson story is how this all took place without a whimper from the African American community. Nobody called him out or his convicted felon of a manager, Don King, for publicly embarrassing their race and prior distinguished champions including Muhammad Ali. I guess they were happy enough having a black man hold the title.

Dennis Rodman, Former NBA Player

One of the hardest-working basketball players to reach the plateau of NBA hall of famer. He did it his way by becoming a ferocious defender and rebounding force (the most difficult and least glorified in that sport). He played on multiple NBA championship teams and contributed to each, but later in his career his longtime selflessness turned into obvious selfish behavior that led to his retirement. He had become a sideshow with his outrageous antics and conflicts on the court. His mantra became, "Hey, look at me, please look at me, I need you to look at me." He became a caricature and was viewed by most people with no racial animus as an unfortunate clown. Dennis had a very tough childhood, and it probably contributed to his current alcohol, drug, and obvious depressive episodes. However, like many other notorious African Americans who become an embarrassment on the national stage, it seems impossible to find a legitimate black leader to say enough of this and get them help.

The fool that he became entered the national political arena when he gushed his admiration for the new dictator of North Korea (the most repressive regime on earth), Kim Jong-un. He began urging President Obama to become more engaged with this wonderful guy and was giving aid and comfort to one of our most hostile enemies. President Obama should have pulled his passport and told him point-blank to cease and desist (to the President's shame, he did not). The final straw came in January of 2014 when Ambassador Rodman sided with the North Korean government and stated publicly that Kenneth Bae, an imprisoned American prisoner of North Korea, had brought on his own problems. That did it, even the American press went into a rage. Ambassador Rodman was now persona non grata in the United States, so what could he do? He took the course of many afflicted scoundrels in the public's eye—he entered rehab. I, for one, hope that he is permanently in rehab because his act was a bad one for his race, his country, and himself.

Tiger Woods, Professional Golfer

I may be a bit schizophrenic, but Mr. Woods wears a black hat too. Tiger has been unfairly attacked by some media people, he has been taken to task by prominent African Americans for not being black enough (code for not being political), and has been resented by a vast number of white Tiger haters for, simply, his race. He has handled all of these situations with class and candor.

Then I was watching TV one morning, and the news story was about his injury from a vehicular crash in his driveway! I said to myself, "Run that by me again." The lid from this trash can exploded into the air. All hell was breaking loose, and day after day more dirt was coming out about (up to that time) a spotless black icon. To summarize, he was guilty of infidelity on a gargantuan scale with strippers, porn stars, and a variety of other less-reputable women. All of his detractors gleefully rubbed their hands with joy. I was dumbfounded. The breadth of the scandal played out for months: it affected his PGA golf schedule, his personal-appearance schedule, and his privacy, but worst of all it made him the subject of derision and even hate from some. It was now open season on Tiger, and he had brought it all on himself. He was not circumspect with his extramarital love life; too many associates knew the truth; and women, yes women, rarely keep their mouths shut.

He has marginally recovered since the divorce from his exceptionally beautiful ex-wife and moved on as a divorced man with a new stunning girlfriend. However, he is no better than anyone else, as I've stated throughout this piece, when it comes to treating women and children badly. His own father was another example of mistreatment of women over an extensive period. Yes, white men are not very good in relationships with women but in the African American community this problem is epidemic. It is unfortunate that a man of Tiger's intellect and self-discipline in golf could have allowed himself to morally collapse in such a manner. He has much to atone for.

Chapter 21:

White Heroes and Villains

HEROES

Juliette Hampton Morgan, Citizen Activist

Ms. Morgan was a wealthy, educated, and socially active resident of Montgomery, Alabama. She was forced to ride buses in that community due to an anxiety condition that prevented her from driving her own car. She was well known in social circles and counted as friends F. Scott Fitzgerald, his wife, Zelda, and actress Tallulah Bankhead.

An incident occurred in 1939 while she was riding on a public bus. The driver consciously abused a black lady and drove off as she tried to enter the rear door as was the custom for black passengers. Juliette pulled the emergency cord and demanded that the black lady be allowed to board the bus. She continued to complain to the Montgomery Bus officials but got only personal abuse for doing so. Remember, this was sixteen years before the Rosa Parks incident that triggered the Montgomery Bus Boycott.

As early as 1952, she wrote the following letter to the Montgomery Advertiser:

> "Are people naïve enough to believe that Negroes are happy, grateful to be pushed around and told they are inferior and told to move on back? They may take it for a long time but not forever."

This was published in the worst period of racial animus since post-Civil War Reconstruction. She made herself a target for retribution regardless of her station in life.

Rosa Parks's refusal to move to the back of the bus occurred on December 1, 1955, and on December 12, 1955, Ms. Morgan wrote again to the *Montgomery Advertiser* to state the following:

"The Negroes of Montgomery seem to have taken a lesson from Gandhi. Their own task is greater than Gandhi's however, for they have greater prejudice to overcome. One feels that history is being made in Montgomery these days. It is hard to imagine a soul so dead, a heart so hard, a vision so blinded and provincial as not to be moved with admiration at the quiet dignity, discipline and dedication with which the Negroes have conducted their boycott."

Juliette Morgan continued her one woman crusade for equal rights and justice, but she reaped scorn, physical threats, a cross burned in her yard, and her job at the public library was lost. She became a victim of anxiety and depression and on July 15, 1957, she took her own life. Her courage, tenacity, and good will toward black people gets little, if any, public mention as a civil rights champion. That is sad indeed.

Dr. Martin Luther King Jr. wrote in his book, *Stride Toward Freedom: The Montgomery Story*:

> "About a week after the protest started, a white woman who understood and sympathized with the Negroes' efforts wrote a letter to the editor of the *Montgomery Advertiser* comparing the bus protest with the Gandhian movement in India. Miss Juliette Morgan, sensitive and frail, did not long survive the rejection and condemnation of the white community, but long before she died in the summer of 1957, the name of Mahatma Gandhi was well known in Montgomery."

Buford Boone, Newspaper Editor

Mr. Boone was an outspoken critic of segregation as a way of life in the South. Juliette Morgan heard of his open opposition to a White Citizens' Council that was promoting segregation with the attendant violence. She wrote the following letter to him, and he courageously published it with her permission on January 14, 1957, in The Tuscaloosa News.

"There are so many Southerners from various walks of life that know you are right. They know what they call our Southern way of life must inevitably change. Many of them are eager for change, but are afraid to express themselves—so afraid to stand alone, to walk out naked as it were. Everyone who speaks as you do, who has the faith to do what he believes right in scorn of the consequences, does great good in preparing the way for a happier and more equitable future for all Americans. You help redeem Alabama's very bad behavior in the eyes of the nation and the world. I had begun to wonder if there were any men in the state—any white men—with any sane evaluation of our situation here in the middle of the twentieth century, with any good will, and most especially with any moral courage to express it."

The term profile in courage seems to suit Buford Boone quite well.

Eleanor Roosevelt, First Lady and Activist

Anna Eleanor Roosevelt was born into wealth, but both of her parents died before she was ten years old. She was also the niece of President Theodore Roosevelt. Her guardian sent her to be educated in an English boarding school that was run by a strong-minded feminist. This provided young Eleanor an opportunity to come out of her shell and exhibit self-confidence.

She married Franklin Delano Roosevelt when she was twenty years old, and the two embraced politics the rest of their lives. Eleanor always bristled at discrimination by gender, religion, or race. She was outspoken when it came to abuses from a humanitarian standpoint, and this caused her husband as president more than simple embarrassment. The first lady could not be muzzled, and one of her strongest concerns was the unequal treatment of black people in the South (which was problematic because these states were strongly in the Democratic Party's voting column).

She broke a long-standing White House tradition of inviting only white people to be guests and literally invited hundreds of African Americans to join her and the president in the people's house. Mrs. Roosevelt heard of a situation when Marian Anderson, the talented black singer, was scheduled to give a concert at Constitution Hall in Washington, D.C., but had that concert cancelled by opposition from the Daughters of the American Revolution. The first lady took it upon herself to reschedule the concert on the steps of the Lincoln Memorial (a quite fitting venue).

The outbreak of World War II brought her more opportunities to become a force for change and conflicts with the white establishment. She heard of the War Department's proposal to create an all-black aviation squadron, and she lent her strong auspices to that reality. In March of 1941 she took the opportunity to fly with one of the Tuskegee Airmen to publicize their unit.

Franklin's death in 1945 did not curtail her voice in politics. No Democrat running for the presidency could do so without properly genuflecting to Eleanor Roosevelt. She continued her humanitarian efforts through the United Nations and her activities for black people in America. She was unbowed by public criticism regardless of the source. To go unrecognized as a major player in the civil rights struggle would be a gross injustice.

President Harry Truman

President Truman was a fair-minded person by all historical accounts, and his integration of the armed forces by an executive order proved that. There is no real quantification of the full effect of that courageous move, but certainly millions of African Americans benefited by the reality of the new equality in the ranks. "Give 'Em Hell, Harry" certainly did just that. You can bet that the president was chided and threatened within his own political party for his action. There was universal condemnation from his "solid South" constituency, but he did what he knew in his heart to be right.

Believe me, I'm not a fan of Harry Truman for a lot of other reasons, but on this issue he deserves all the credit in the world. What happened to black servicemen in and immediately after World War II was just horrible. People agree that Vietnam veterans were treated badly upon coming home but how about African Americans who came back to one notch above slavery in 1945? I have stated earlier that black people that I served with were the equal of white soldiers, but that might never have come to pass if the generals, admirals, and congressmen had their way. Is this event commemorated anywhere in our schools today?

Charlton Heston, Actor and Activist

A man who was outrageously savaged by leftists over his stand on the sanctity of the Second Amendment (the right to bear arms) to the US Constitution was a champion of African American human rights before it was fashionable in Hollywood. Mr. Heston is another of those people who had been a strong supporter of the Democratic Party who became a Republican out of disenchantment with the extreme left's agenda and control. He was a prominent figure associated with Dr. King's March on Washington in 1963 (not exactly a film career booster at the time). From 1965 to 1971 he was the president of the Screen Actors Guild (conservatives could never be elected), but by 1971 he was in constant battle with Ed Asner who we all now know not as Lou Grant of the Mary Tyler Moore Show but as a premier leftist who doesn't like much of America.

Charlton Heston was his own man, and he quarreled with many on the far right as a Republican over the need to achieve a color blind society as espoused by Dr. King. His character was unimpeachable and his moral courage was unmatched.

Dick Clark

This man's nickname was "America's Oldest Teenager". In 1957 he took over a Philadelphia television station's musical variety show that had been renamed American Bandstand. This show brought rock and roll music into the nation's homes. He personally desegregated the show's all white artist policy adding black entertainers and audience participants. it became a daily blockbuster for the ABC television network. He blew the doors off for black musical talent to get national attention for the first time. I believe that he was loved by all people regardless of race.

Howard Cosell, Lawyer and Sports Journalist

His assessment of himself was "arrogant, pompous, obnoxious, vain, cruel, verbose, a show-off," Yet he changed sports journalism forever with these not-very-endearing attributes. The name Howard Cosell could drive sports fans into a rage. I sincerely believe (based on my own experiences) that his detractors far outnumbered his supporters. Sports reporters literally hated him and his persona.

Then along came Cassius Clay, a very talented boxer with the tag of "the Louisville Lip" for his braggadocio and humor. Howard somehow became a part of the promotion aspects of Clay's early victories as a professional heavyweight. He asked tough, direct questions of the champ but could be playful as well. The two were made for each other and made history together.

Cassius became associated with the Nation of Islam after he became the world champion in 1964 and was vilified by the media while Cosell defended his constitutional right to do so. Then in 1967, when Muhammad Ali refused military induction, Howard was one of very few who not only understood his action but intelligently defended it. The national media raked both of them with vitriol that makes today's political commentary look mild.

The Olympic Games were held in Mexico City in 1968, and nobody remembers who won what, but two black men made history. They stood on the stand to receive their medals but raised their black gloved fists (a sign of black power) during the playing of America's national anthem. All hell broke loose in the US with a wave of white indignation, but Howard Cosell was an unabashed supporter. Many tried to assert that Cosell's stances were calculated and cynical, but one look at his background would refute that premise. He was Jewish and raised in Brooklyn, New York; therefore, it could be assumed that he witnessed discrimination firsthand, thus his empathy for African Americans and their horrific treatment.

Howard was along for the ride again when Muhammad Ali had his appeal that the US Supreme Court reverse his conviction. He broadcast all but one of Ali's fights upon his return to boxing in 1970. The two had so many memorable interviews that it is in your best interest to see and hear them on YouTube yourselves. Cosell was one of a kind.

Gregory Peck, Actor

Mr. Peck was one of the finest actors of all time, but it is one role that gets him on this honor roll (at least mine). Harper

Lee, a daughter of Alabama, wrote a searing best-selling novel about her childhood called *To Kill a Mockingbird* that won the Pulitzer Prize. A movie was later released based on the book with the same title.

Gregory Peck played the pivotal role as Atticus Finch, a lawyer and widowed father with two young children, who was appointed to defend a black farmhand accused of raping a white woman. His portrayal is still with me now because of his soulful delivery of so many human emotions. He not only defends Tom Robinson, but he clearly demonstrates his innocence through a withering cross-examination of the accuser. Atticus is as shattered as the defendant when the all-white male jury returns a guilty verdict. Throughout the trial Atticus is threatened and subjected to abuse in his community, but he provides the best possible representation, well beyond what could be expected, for Tom. Then the sky falls on the audience with the information that Tom Robinson has been shot and killed "while trying to escape."

A short time later, the Finch children, while returning home from a costume party, are attacked by the husband of the accuser in the trial, and he is killed in a struggle by the Finch's neighbor, Boo Radley, a mentally retarded soul with great strength.

The book and movie left an indelible impression of the injustice that existed at the time but also in the 1960s in the same deep South. Many white people even today do not wish to be reminded of the many black men who were lynched by the Klan or the Southern justice system for black people. I recommend that they consider that no other race in this country was ever subjected to the systematic, legalized violence as black people were.

Schwerner and Goodman, Civil Rights Workers

On the evening of June 21, 1964, three young civil rights workers were murdered in cold blood by members of the Mississippi White Knights of the Ku Klux Klan. Two of these men were Michael Schwerner (twenty-four) and Andrew Goodman (twenty). Both were New Yorkers with a passion for enabling black people in Mississippi to vote. The third was James Earl Chaney (twenty-one) an African American Mississippi native.

The heinous nature of these murders was such that they were taken into police custody over a flat tire in Philadelphia, Mississippi and then turned over by police to their fellow Klansmen for execution. The bodies of all three were found on August 4, 1964, under an earthen dam. The two white guys were Jewish, as were many other Jews heavily involved in the civil rights movement. Are there any lasting tributes to the Schwerners and Goodmans by the African American community? No, today there are ongoing insults by the Jacksons, the Sharptons, and the Farrakhans. It is as if the civil rights movement was of only African Americans, by only African Americans, and for African Americans. It is a disheartening outcome for legitimate brotherhood.

George Carlin, Comedian

A one-man storm of comedy, Mr. Carlin presented humor in almost every subject that can come to mind. He never acted as a star but rather as this somewhat goofy fellow who wanted to make people laugh.

I remember watching him one night when he spoke of the influence that black people had over white people (unimaginable, right?) without the white people knowing it.

The piece went like this. You put nine black people in one room for one week with a single white person. At the end of the week you can guarantee that the white guy speaks, dresses, and acts like the black brothers. Phase two of the experiment calls for a simple reversal of the numbers, now one black man and nine white guys together in a room for one week. The result is that the nine white dudes all exhibit the same mannerisms and dialect of the single black man. When I heard this I readily accepted that notion.

Today men's and boys' fashion statements, when it comes to sports hats, sneakers, pants (baggy and falling off one's butt), and jeans, are driven by African American adopted style. Exhibit A is the white dude walking down the street with jeans shorts that are at least two waist sizes too big, preferably so his underwear shows, the bottom of the shorts extended down to about twelve inches above his feet, his sneakers untied, and wearing an oversized baseball cap backward with a nondescript shirt. He is telling the world that he is cool and thinks that he did this all on his own.

Norman Lear, Television Writer and Producer

Norman Lear led a revolution in the 1970s for black participation in mainstream television. All in the Family debuted on January 12, 1971, to severe criticism and poor ratings (it would cause convulsions today with the politically correct crowd), but it survived and later flourished as the number one show on television for five years. It demonstrated bigotry in the form of an uneducated, opinionated, and racist New Yorker named Archie Bunker. The neighbors of this Neanderthal, the Jefferson family, just happened to be black and owned a successful cleaning store. George Jefferson, the equally bigoted black father and husband, portrayed racist animus to white people in general. Who could imagine that such a show would transcend traditional silence in these matters to make the point that racists are often simply stupid? The same people who loved Archie could see the error of his ways, and they could recognize people in their own circle with similar views as his. The writing was clever, entertaining, and bold for network television.

The success of *All in the Family* emboldened Norman Lear to produce a more black-oriented show that became a sensational hit. *Sanford and Son* opened on January 14, 1972, and introduced America's television audience to Redd Foxx, the irascible, bigoted junk dealer in South Central Los Angeles. His son, played by Demond Wilson, was the counterbalance. The show came at the viewer with a black perspective not seen before. Redd Foxx stated in an early episode that "there isn't anything uglier than a ninety-year-old white woman." It drew laughs as did most of the material on their show. Redd became an overnight sensation after doing comedy in clubs and on explicit sexual records for the previous twenty years. He proved that a black star could be more than viable in the television markets (the show is still on in syndication forty years later).

Lear went on to produce two other black-based successful television shows: *The Jeffersons*, a spin-off from *All in the Family* and *Good Times*, which was about a black family living in the Cabrini-Green project in Chicago. The latter helped the careers of Jimmie Walker, Esther Rolle, and John Amos. That show presented a poor black family trying to overcome adversity through hard work and tenacity.

So nineteen years after *Amos and Andy* was hounded off the air, Norman Lear gave America four shows with black actors playing prominent roles and receiving acclaim for their work. His work taught us lessons about our mutual needs to respect each other, and now forty years later the race climate has deteriorated to levels back in the 1960s.

Group Award for the Many Producers of Black Sitcoms

Wikipedia lists 144 black sitcoms from 1950, as discussed above, through 2013. Some of the more notable are:

- *The Fresh Prince of Bel-Air*
- *Family Matters*
- *House of Payne*
- *Martin*
- *A Different World*
- *The Bernie Mac Show*
- *Different Strokes*
- *Sister, Sister*
- *Gimme a Break!*
- *The Steve Harvey Show*
- *The Jamie Foxx Show*
- *The Hughleys*
- *Benson*
- *Webster*
- *The Sinbad Show*
- *Bustin' Loose*
- *The Gregory Hines Show*
- *Wanda at Large*

President Ronald Reagan

The first president to name an African American, Gen. Colin Powell, to be his national security adviser, and General Powell later served as Secretary of State in two other Republican administrations. This president succeeded the Jimmy Carter administration that was a disaster in economic and foreign policy. President Reagan brought the country to economic prosperity that provided jobs to all including African Americans, and he brought US prestige abroad to new heights with the end of the Cold War with the Soviet Union. He cared not what the race of any man was but judged all by their character.

VILLAINS

Group Award to All Police Departments That Discriminated in the Application of the Law

This is the most despicable of all racist actions. Ever since the Emancipation Proclamation, African Americans were victimized solely due to their skin color. Incidents of murders, beatings, and lynchings were commonplace in the South with law enforcement complicit before, during, or after the acts. People like Bull Connor, the commissioner of public safety in Birmingham, Alabama, created the horrific pictures of unleashed attack dogs and high-pressure fire hoses against a peaceful march of black folks in 1963.

Since then there have been more subtle examples of police brutality for fifty years, and they continue today. Black people have been shot over twenty times by police fearing for their safety, and the departments have been loath to investigate and punish their own. This has led to a total mistrust of police throughout the country on the part of African Americans. It has truly been a war against people of color and will continue unless police are reined in. I have had a personal experience of police abuse in spite of never having been arrested, so I can imagine how bad it is for African

Americans and Hispanics. One need not look any farther than the FBI under the tyrannical J. Edgar Hoover who even blackmailed presidents that were his superiors.

Jerry Springer, Television Host

A very, very smart guy who has had success in broadcasting but chose to go after the gold in television ratings in 1994 with a new format. He and his producers embarked on a show based on sexual promiscuity, freakish sexual appetites, and general sleaziness. America's lowest common denominator in taste assured his achieving his goal of stardom on a national stage with economic rewards as well. His in studio audience now routinely includes identified college students.

The problem that I have with Jerry is the disproportionate share of African American and Hispanic guests who are skewered daily for stereotypical sexual behaviors: men mistreating spouses or baby mamas, women who are uneducated and more frequently jobless without a clue, and transsexuals preying on black men holding them up to public ridicule. It is a nightmare for people of color because in a sick way these creatures get their ten minutes of fame. The show in this guise of helping people through Jerry's final thoughts at the end of each program is a continuing hit with little open criticism from black leadership. I wonder why! The stereotypes are as graphic as anything can be.

There is only one winner here and that's Jerry.

Maury Povich, Television Host

Mr. Povich is bright, articulate, personable, and a former television journalist. In 1998 he bought into the trashiest television ever with *Maury*, which deals with identifying fathers of illegitimate children through paternity tests. The disproportionality of race in the mix does not seem to bother Maury a bit. The free-for-all atmosphere is similar to Springer but without the physical attacks. It is the type of show that the movie *Network* envisioned for the sole benefit of ratings and money for the host and producers.

Again, there is no hue and cry to rid this racist element from black leadership. The show is in a time slot conducive to stay-at-home moms who can live vicariously as superior to those they watch. There is no lesson to be learned because now in its sixteenth year there is no lack of guests. The illegitimacy rate among African American and Hispanic women assures plenty of candidates into the future.

Maury is now seventy-five and still milking every penny. I hope that he is satisfied with his estimated salary of $14 million per year for publicly humiliating his "guests."

Group Award for Network News

CBS, NBC, and ABC have a few things in common, but their cowardice in avoiding significant African American problems is shameful. These are supposed to be the best at their craft. Please tell me when was the last time they took anyone on a tour of the worst city schools (elementary through high school)? When did they discover horrific black-on-black shootings, crime and murders (I believe it was when Chicago black deaths over a period of time exceeded Afghanistan)? Why no coverage of the black homeless problems? They've always made a point of those left behind during Republican administrations. Where is the first African American anchor of the evening news? They are always about equality in the workplace, but it seems to be a "do as I say" and not a "do as I do" approach (blatant hypocrisy). Why no spotlight investigations into the drug lords of New York who target primarily black poor people? Why no exposure of the black unemployment rates to include black teen unemployment?

There is a simple answer to all of the above: either they really do not care about the downtrodden among us, or they are too lazy to do their jobs of reporting *the news*. I take the position that it is a combination of both. There was a time when reporting news shaped public opinion, but now there are truly sinister forces at work that determine what is newsworthy for our interest. I guess their concern for African Americans is satisfied when MSNBC, a poor facsimile of a cable affiliate of NBC, puts Al Sharpton on the air each night. Wonderful!

Rep. John Boehner, Speaker of the House of Representatives.

I have seen many Republican Speakers of the House over my sixty-nine years, but this character is without question the worst. He has not only disappointed conservative Republicans and conservative independents, but he will go down in history as the least visionary and courageous person to hold that high office.

He and his Republican colleagues had a tremendous opportunity to slay the Republican anti-black dragon. They were in a position to pass a school voucher plan that would have been anathema to people like Harry Reid, the majority leader in the senate, and President Obama as well. It would have shown concern and compassion for the oppressed in our failing public education system. Instead they opted for useless votes on repealing Obamacare when all they had to do was allow it to collapse under its own weight, which it is doing right now.

Their stance on immigration reform at the behest of the US Chamber of Commerce is an insult to all working Americans. So he and his cronies in the Republican leadership continue to be equal-opportunity disappointments to black and white alike.

Labor Unions

Labor unions are and have been the backbone of the Democratic Party. Yet almost ninety years after the railroad sleeping car porters organized in 1925, this backbone has not one major union headed by a black or African American. As of 2010, 20 percent of black workers were union members enjoying a 36 percent higher median salary over non-union black workers. Trade unions in particular and the American Federation of Labor, in particular, had a long-standing opposition to black membership into the 1970s (except for the base labor jobs with low pay scales). The old canard was that they didn't have the mental or physical capacity for union labor. We knew from the World War II experience that such a position only marked deep-seated racism from rank-and-file members and their leaders. To their credit today, all unions are civil rights activists because they ultimately discovered that a unified labor force was good for achieving their political and membership goals.

African Americans would have been much farther down their road to human dignity and freedom had this late enlightenment occurred much sooner. A. Philip Randolph, the head of the Brotherhood of Sleeping Car Porters (an all-black union), was a leader for equality in the labor force, and in 1941 he threatened a march on Washington to protest the segregationist policies of the US government. President Franklin D. Roosevelt was forced to acquiesce to some of

Randolph's demands to avoid a horrible embarrassment. However many of the expected gains were sabotaged by the US Congress withholding funds to enforce statutes from Roosevelt's executive orders. World War II was followed by more racial animus by most trade unions and only federal legislation saved the day for the black labor force.

It should be noted that the black or African American labor participation rate increased to an all-time high from a baseline of 60 percent in 1975 to 66.5 percent in 1998. It is down to 60.8 percent in 2014 with an African American president, an African American attorney general and a Democrat-controlled congress fully supporting labor unions!

Donald Sterling, Lawyer and NBA Team Owner

Last but not least, we have the new racist star of the moment. This man is devoid of any human redeeming value by any fair standard. Yes, he is a self-made multimillionaire, but his personal history shows that he even legally changed his name Tokowitz to Sterling for financial reasons (Tokowitz was Jewish, and he doubted he could succeed in business with such identification). His fortune allowed him to treat most people as inferior, but he took delight in racial stereotyping in particular (which was later proven in court).

In 1981 he bought the San Diego Clippers NBA franchise, an odd choice for someone with serious issues with black people. He then proceeded to starve the team financially for about twenty years. He was brought to housing court on complaints of racial discrimination. The court ordered payment of attorneys' fees in the amount of 4.9 million dollars, and the eighteen plaintiffs in the case agreed to an out-of-court settlement. Then in 2006 he was sued *again*, this time by the US Justice Department for blatant discrimination in filling vacant apartments to almost anybody but African Americans and Hispanics. This prompted Mr. Sterling to pay another 2.7 million dollars in fines and an agreed settlement with victims. Then in 2009 he was sued by one of the greatest players in NBA history, Elgin Baylor, for employment discrimination on the basis of age and race, and this suit has been dropped by Mr. Baylor. Lastly, we have a sexual harassment suit filed in 1996 that was settled confidentially in 1998. *What a guy!*

The NBA, however, did not seem to take notice of any of the racial complaints against their club owner until his racial animus was caught on tape by his less than his honorable mistress. It appears that her free ride was coming to an end, and she set him up (birds of a feather). Now the NBA came out with guns blazing to "get rid of this pariah in their midst" as if there are no other snakes in their woodpile. Remember this is almost an entire league of black people (African American players comprised 76.3 percent of the total), and majority owners are but 2 percent of these thirty teams. The league touts its "splendid record" for hiring African American general managers and coaches as rated against other professional sports teams! Truth is that in the 2012 to 2013 season, African American general managers held 23.3 percent of those jobs, and African American coaches held 43.3 percent of total NBA coaching positions. Is this really the era of NBA enlightenment? They're doing great in contrast to the National Hockey League minority hiring record!

Here is the ultimate kicker. This same Donald Sterling, it turns out, is a two-time awardee of the Los Angeles Chapter of the NAACP for lifetime achievement purportedly based on serious cash contributions (the second award was revoked after the firestorm of his comments hit the fan). This type of hypocrisy is not new to this organization, and if most people do not know this, they should wake up soon.

Chapter 22:

The Specter of Ferguson

Ferguson, Missouri, until recently, was a nondescript town of 21,111 people. It is now the crucible of race relations in America because on August 19 2014, Michael Brown was shot and killed by a Ferguson police officer named Darren Wilson. As of today we know certain *facts*:

*Michael Brown was 6' 4" tall and weighed 292 pounds.

- He was eighteen at the time of his death.
- He had just robbed a store before he encountered Police Officer Darren Wilson, who had been made aware of a recent robbery in his sector. Wilson saw two men matching the robbery suspects walking in the middle of the street, and that's where the altercation began.

- Wilson told the two suspects to go to the curb. A scuffle between Michael and the officer began immediately, and Officer Wilson struggled to keep his gun from Mr. Brown's attempt to take it from him. Officer Wilson's gun was discharged twice within his patrol car (this was clearly corroborated by DNA and other forensic evidence). Officer Wilson sustained abrasions to his face during that scuffle.
- Michael Brown died from gunshot wounds in several areas of his torso. The version of the shooting by Michael Brown's accomplice that Mr. Brown was shot in the back and then was shot in cold blood with his hands up was thoroughly debunked by forensics and African American testimony that agreed with Darren Wilson's account of the events.

These are not in dispute today, but ever since the day of the shooting, forces have been marshalled to protest the murder of Michael Brown. These included television network commentators, politicians, an irresponsible governor of the State of Missouri and the usual suspects in such conflicts: the New Black Panther Party, Al Sharpton, and Jesse Jackson. This racial cocktail had been brewing from day one with threats of racial riots and harm to some in the white communities in the area including the city of St. Louis, Missouri.

The protests at the outset in August turned violent quickly, and that resulted in significant damage to businesses, some of which were owned by black people and were fomented by people from well outside the greater St. Louis community. It is unfortunate that riots like this going back to the sixties have disadvantaged black people much more than whites. I truly believe that some would really like to see white bloodshed to satisfy their anger and hatred. Remember that it was the parents of Trayvon Martin who called for peace after their son's killer was acquitted on a politically motivated charge of second-degree murder, which was unsustainable by the facts. Worse of all, the Attorney General of the United States interjected himself, while representing President Obama, into this cauldron at the obvious behest of his president. He did not preach calm but rather acted as an advocate for the Brown family without a full knowledge of the facts.

The facts as cited here are now in. I now know that Officer Brown has been vindicated by a grand jury that included three African Americans. I know that this is a country that is supposed to be about the rule of law. The mantra of the Ferguson riots that followed Mr. Brown's death were based on a premise that Mr. Brown was kneeling with his hands raised above his head when he was shot several times by the police officer. We now have heard from Attorney General Holder that such a scenario has been totally refuted by his own U.S. Justice Department's seven month investigation. I wonder how all those black athletes and congressional black congress people feel now about their rush to judgment that enflamed the racial divide in this country. The apology silence is deafening. Riots are anarchy, and the costs to all citizens are high, but composure and vetting of the accurate facts in this case should be color blind. These incidents are a reminder of how racially polarized this nation has become and summarize the unfortunate fact that African Americans continue to hold on to victimization by white people and particularly white police regardless of facts.

Chapter 23:

Reconciliation

This exercise has been rewarding for me because I learned about black history as never before. Some of the research was enlightening as to the significant numbers of African Americans that championed civil and human rights while being willing to sacrifice even their lives in this cause. The notion that slavery is a root cause for the poor overall state of black America is absurd on its face. It is a lingering, feeble excuse for the shiftless, uneducated, drug-infected, and violent minority to lay on white society. Liberals love guilt when it comes to sins of the nation, and they disparage those serious African Americans who espouse education and a serious work ethic. I recently watched a CNN interview of Morgan Freeman, the great black actor, by Don Lemon of CNN, who also happened to be black. Mr. Lemon inquired of Mr. Freeman whether he thought that young African Americans were victims in today's society. His answer was simple. "You and I are here now because of education and hard work, and we both know that's bullshit." Bit by bit, prominent black citizens are no longer accepting the old canard about slavery holding back their fellow African American brothers and sisters from succeeding in America. They look at the current American landscape and find a president, an attorney general, lawyers, doctors, media people, scholars, scientists, sports superstars, and other brothers and sisters in every other endeavor. Yet the hand-wringers continue to be trotted out by the leftist media to spew their venom against white people. The same media that wastes valuable airtime on the twentieth anniversary of O. J. Simpson's acquittal rather than insight into the failing public school system tries to tell us how to think about race.

It has been fifty years since the enactment of the Civil Rights Legislation of 1964. There have been incredible racial injustices that have occurred since, but to continue to fail to recognize the achievements of African American people through the basics of hard work and education is a path to nowhere for young inner-city black youth. The carnage of drug violence in almost every major city in America must be blamed rightfully on the destruction of the black family unit through the liberal panacea of more and more welfare types of assistance. Crime against fellow innocent black people should be called what it is, a scourge of black lawlessness. Black religious leaders should shout from the rooftops that black girls and women should respect themselves sexually and not seize the brass ring of supposed independence through illegitimate children and welfare subsidies. Every black person in a leadership position should stress the importance of a good education and yes a voucher system to escape horrible public schools. In the documentary *Waiting for Superman*, a school superintendent is totally hostile to the notion of charter school successes. Then when he is asked about his own education, he readily confesses that he was a product of Catholic private schools. Dr. Martin Luther King's famous speech during the 1963 March on Washington spoke of a true color-blind society, and today we still have black antagonists holding on to the failed policies of the past to bring a brighter future (true madness). The song "We Shall Overcome" sung that same day by blacks and whites alike has been dismissed by the race hustlers out there with their own motto of "blacks can't overcome."

I currently live in Florida, and wherever you look, there are manual laborers doing all kinds of painstaking work: roofing, landscaping, road engineering, etc., and the vast majority are Hispanic. They are happy to be employed, and when seen at the local Publix supermarkets they pay by cash with their young families in tow. They have a language problem and certainly look different from your average white person, but they come here with nothing and are sought by employers (I understand that the employer may be hiring illegals and paying less than the fair wage due to their status) and look for a better future for their families. They are the most vulnerable among us, but they show up every day and work very, very hard in ninety-degree heat. These people have chosen the paths of most of our immigrants of the past be they Poles, Chinese, Irish, Slavs, Greeks, French Canadians, Vietnamese, Cambodians, Laotians, Indians, Pakistanis, or Russians. Why would this not be the expected route for success by African Americans? Please don't tell me that employers are all racist. Money talks, and good workers are always in demand.

The predominantly leftist media needs to take a real look at their complicity in supporting totally discredited government policies that have brought human conditions in inner-city black communities to desperation. Their voice should use its power to call out the abject failures so obvious to most common-sense practitioners. Television news should get back to its roots and present facts rather than entertainment for ratings purposes. Everyone knows that good news is not relevant to news organizations, but it would be helpful if they would focus on the Marva Collins types. Wouldn't it be refreshing for us to see where the money in public education in our major cities is going on a national network? I don't know about you, but I'm very tired of seeing the same talking heads telling us their views on what's going on and what should be done. I am equally fed up with partisanship presented as news. I am conservative, but it does the Fox Network little good when it trots out the likes of Karl Rove, Dana Perino, Dick Cheney, and other George W. Bush acolytes to discuss current political issues (their credibility is zero).

I am not a devoutly religious person, but I do believe in God. We are at a point in history where godlessness and immorality have reached critical mass. The populace is insensitive to horrific musical lyrics, drug-related deaths, a corrupt justice system, and political malfeasance at all levels. We shrink from confrontation even to protect families from violence. We watch inane television without real storylines or with a guarantee of weekly gratuitous sex and violence. There is no longer any respect for family viewing by networks or cable. It is odd that, only thirteen years after the attacks on 9/11 when people ran to churches, we see the media routinely ridicule Christians and Orthodox Jews while daring not to freely discuss the Islamist nature of terrorism. It is a bit like *Alice in Wonderland*. Issues that should worry each and every one of us, black and white, are dismissed by average people: the IRS used as a tool against political opponents, the release of five Taliban fanatics to secure a deserter under the pretext of a prisoner swap, the NSA scandal, lack of any Southern border security, the highest rate of joblessness (based on the labor participation rate established long ago without the current gimmicks), and lower wages since President Obama took office. I expect that not too far in the future Americans will be back on their knees praying to a God that they have ignored most of their lives. Chaos and decline are here today, and the young among us say "What, me worry?" from *MAD* magazine, founded in the 1950s.

I hope that what I have presented has been instructive.

Epilogue

This treatise was an attempt to examine the realities of my own life within the context of racial encounters. The overwhelming concern in my writing this book has been the improvement of African Americans through improved educational opportunities and self-study. I presented several black people throughout history who have been cornerstones of the fight for equality. I have condemned the race hustlers for who and what they are, a negative counterbalance to progress. The notion that black women can continue their roles as "baby mamas" with irresponsible black or white men with impunity is ludicrous.

The ongoing blame on "the Man" (understood to be the white man) as the source of the failures of black America belies the successes of black people in every field of endeavor including the presidency of the United States. Do you remember the media disparagement of low-paying jobs at McDonald's for black people? They seem worthwhile to the blacks, whites, and Hispanics that man those positions today!

Self-respect for his brothers and sisters was the goal of Malcolm X, and he and many others gave their lives to that ideal. Dr. King was never concerned with his fame or fortune, and he made a lasting impression on people of every race and creed. They worked every day and never accepted the status quo as a reasonable option. There are no more Malcolms or Dr. Kings, and the tenor of today's activists is more about racial divide, gender, and class warfare at the expense of reason, brotherhood, and mutual respect.

If America is to survive, racial harmony is a critical piece of that puzzle. Unfortunately, we seem to be on the eve of the destruction of racial harmony because of a shooting in Ferguson, Missouri, where a coalition of black activists insist that the law in the case of Michael Brown be bent to their demands of an indictment for murder and subsequent guilty verdict for the police officer involved. It feels eerily the same as white people's demands for the acquittal of Klansmen in Philadelphia, Mississippi, that horrible summer when two white civil rights workers and one black civil rights worker were shot and killed and buried in an earthen dam. The outcome should be determined by the evidence and the law as it is applied and not by the emotions of the moment.

I make no excuses for past sins and racists that exist today because there will always be racists among us of all races. People who hold on to grievances hurt themselves in the long run, and to quote a PBS television series, keeping one's "eyes on the prize" is essential to overcoming obstacles.

We can overcome.

About the Author

I was born in 1945 to a mother, who was a textile mill worker and a father, who was a union structural ironworker. They were first generation Americans.

I was educated in Roman Catholic schools and served as an altar boy throughout grammar school where I learned the importance of religion. I was 16 when my father died in a car crash on his way to work. He was killed when he and two other ironworkers were crushed to death by a Trailways bus (he was 41). As a result, my mother went into a deep depression from his sudden death. Our source of income dropped precipitously to Social Security benefits with minimal assistance from extended family. We ultimately received a settlement of $21,500 from the bus company that was clearly at fault with $10,000 of that sum set aside in trust for higher education costs for my brother and me. This was my introduction to corporate largesse and union brotherhood. My father had been a 22 year union man but because his dues book was not paid up at the time of his death we received NOTHING from the International Ironworkers Union.

I went on to Boston College and graduated in 1967 with a BA in economics. Two days after commencement instead of moving on with my life; I was drafted into the US Army. At the time, I was supporting both my mother and younger brother on what I was making as an ironworker. I served my country proudly in Vietnam as a cobra helicopter gunship pilot in 1970-1971.

I was discharged from the military on April 20 1972, and returned to everyday civilian life. My first steady job was as a claims representative with the Social Security Administration. My total government civil service lasted thirteen and a half years and was marked by frustration in seeing the widowed, disabled, and retired treated in a less than a dignified manner. There were constant struggles with management and subordinates over delivering timely, honest, and fair representation. This culminated in my decision to resign in 1987.

My experience working at Social Security prompted me to attempt to start my own business representing the disabled in attaining benefits due. This endeavor failed because of a lack of steady clients. At the same time, I had been assisting friends as a property manager for ten inner city rental units. Besides the above I held a variety of previous occupations. They ranged in scope: mill worker, hotel desk clerk, postal service letter carrier, municipal garbage worker, substitute school teacher and salesman. I was no blushing rose and learned at the school of hard knocks and I not only survived but thrived.

Through simple dumb luck, I was introduced to someone who offered me a decent, well-paying job as a collections specialist for his building products company. This ultimately led to a permanent position with the company as a credit manager. Over the next 23 years, this person became a great friend as well as my boss. My career expanded exponentially with his support and promotions with the parent company. Eventually my final assignment positioned me to oversee credit operations for 26 district branches throughout the northeast and into the mid-west. I retired in January of 2010.

I have three wonderful children: Elizabeth, Jeffrey and Brian and two adorable grandchildren: Jackson and Nicholas.